THE MAGNIFICENT GLASS GLOBE

N. R. BERGESON

THE MAGNIFICENT GLASS GLOBE by N.R. Bergeson
All rights reserved. Published in the United States of America by Month9Books, LLC.
No part of this book may be used or reproduced in any manner whatsoever without written permission of the publisher, except in the case of brief quotations embodied in critical articles and reviews.

Trade Paperback ISBN: 978-1-945107-81-8
ePub ISBN: 978-1-945107-26-9
Mobipocket ISBN: 978-1-945107-27-6

Published by Tantrum Books for Month9Books, Raleigh, NC 27609
Cover design by Danielle Doolittle

For Ellen (1985-2016) - a steadfast cultural bridge builder.

CHAPTER ONE

Hide and Seek in the Museum

"We're ready," Mary said, as she and Helen adopted running stances.

Ike turned to the wall and covered his eyes.

"ONE!" he counted aloud.

With that signal, Mary took off, running at full speed across the museum. Her best friend jogged alongside with ease. No matter that they were the same age—Helen's long, athletic body was the reason others often mistook the eleven-year old for a teenager.

"… Two … Three … four!"

"You keep going," Helen whispered.

From the corner of her eye, Mary watched Helen disappear

as she veered into the African pottery exhibit. Mary pushed ahead, her kinky dark hair bouncing as she went.

A feeling of unexpected pleasure bubbled up inside her as she ran. A broad grin spread from ear to ear.

Now's the time, she thought. It'd been a while since this feeling had last come.

She closed her eyes briefly, imagining the place she longed to see above all others. As she reopened them, the marble floor turned to dirt beneath her feet. The white walls of the museum sprang forth into lush greenery as leaves and vines covered them. The transition took only seconds, and soon Mary was no longer running through the museum.

She was back, flying on her feet through the rainforest. It really had been too long.

"Ha ha!" she laughed, upping her speed a notch.

Mary felt free and fearless, leaping over fallen logs as she bounded through the jungle. Glancing to the left, she saw two lanky monkeys, swinging from branch to branch and hooting excitedly as they matched her speed. The air felt steamy, and beautiful rainforest noises echoed all around.

Mary turned sharply to her right, rounding a wide tree. Ike would never find her now.

An unexpected light appeared in front of her eyes, catching her off guard.

Huh? she wondered.

And with that momentary, out-of-place thought, it was over. The trees around her vanished, returning to the dull, darkened corridors of the museum.

"No!" she cried in despair. "Come back!"

Mary tried to pretend otherwise, but this adventure hadn't been real.

"I'm in the Amazon. I'm *in* the Amazon," she urged herself, straining to get the engine of her imagination to turn over.

It was no use. Whatever had been working before was gone now. All she could conjure up were vague images, like black-and-white photographs that vanished into smoke before she could get a good look at them.

I'm probably getting too old for this, she thought. She'd be twelve soon, after all. Did all imaginations stop working at twelve? Without hers, who would she be?

It's all because I've been spoiled.

Spoiled by the museum. Not that she'd change anything. She likely wouldn't have formed her imagination in the first place if not for this place. As the curator's daughter, she'd practically grown up here. But maybe it'd caused an overload. The fires of her mind burned too hot, and she'd used up the finite amount of imagined adventure her brain had to offer.

3

Mary reluctantly accepted, yet again, that the museum was only a museum. Not the real thing. Just a place that could provide glimpses of what she might find in faraway places. Places that weren't here, where she was, and probably always would be.

"Ready or not, here I come!" Ike called from the distant wing of the empty museum.

Oh yeah, she remembered. *Hide and seek.*

Mary began looking for a place to hide. Ahead, that light which had yanked her out of the rainforest shone brightly. It took a moment to realize what it was. As she did, her spirit swelled, and her smile returned.

"My lucky day," she said, walking toward the light.

She might not be able to will her imagination back, but Mary knew another way to get the results she craved. It kind of felt like cheating, but at this point, she'd take what she could get.

In front of Mary was her favorite thing in the whole museum. The beautiful world map, illuminated by the spotlight, hung proudly on the corridor wall.

Almost immediately, she felt that familiar tugging sensation. The black-and-white photographs didn't vanish right away. She sighed in satisfaction. There it was.

Faraway places.

Adventures. All thanks to the map.

The rest of what the museum had to offer might be losing its potency, but the map was still an effective way to stimulate the imagination. Something about it, and all maps for that matter, could always draw her in.

Nearly ten feet high and twenty feet wide, the stunning map filled the entire wall. It showed the world in amazing detail. It even had pictures of plants and animals lining its border. Each was connected to a spot on the map by a red line, indicating the native habitat of the plant or animal. As always, Mary dreamed that simply touching the map could magically whisk her away to any place she desired. She wouldn't need her imagination then. Then she'd have it all right in front of her.

In the back of her mind, Mary again remembered the game of hide and seek.

Just another minute, she told herself. It would take her little brother a while to find her, especially since he wouldn't come looking in these darkened exhibits alone. She had time.

And she needed this.

One bright picture caught her eye, as it had countless times before. A large, spotted cat climbed along a green log in an even greener jungle. She looked at the description and read:

The Amazon jaguar (Panthera onca onca) is one of the largest predators living in the rainforest basin. Accurate numbers are difficult to estimate, but they are very rare, and seldom seen by humans.

A line connected the picture to the heart of the Amazon. Reaching up, Mary traced it with her finger.

"Right there," she said, tapping her finger in the middle of the rainforest. "That's where I want to go."

Her mind's eye began to produce the rainforest once again, as creeper vines sprung from the surface of the map and wrapped around her wrist. The melody of chanting birds and monkeys filled the air.

Deep down, Mary understood the solution to her problem. She had for a while. Her imagination wasn't dying. It'd only matured, just as she had. Babies could live on milk, but as they got older, they needed more variety in their diet. Her younger imagination could produce the adventure she craved when fed by the interesting artifacts of the museum, but it needed something more now.

She needed to be fed the real thing.

This was why she'd been begging her parents for the chance to *really* go somewhere. To keep her imagination alive and healthy.

"Yes, I think it would be an interesting place too," said an unexpected voice from behind.

Mary yelped as she spun around, startled by the intruder. All traces of her imagined rainforest vanished yet again.

"I'm sorry, I didn't mean to frighten you," apologized the janitor.

The tall, aging man pushed a wide broom across the floor. His white hair was trimmed short and neat, much like his narrow white mustache. It matched his pale skin. Mary had seen him before, but had never spoken to him. He hadn't been working at the museum for long.

"So, you like to travel?" the janitor asked, revealing his slight accent.

She tried to remember the man's name.

"Yes, well, I think so," Mary stammered, her heart still racing from the fright he'd given her. "I've never actually gone anywhere."

"And why the Amazon?" asked the janitor. "You like hot weather?"

"I don't know," Mary said. "Maybe because there's more life in the Amazon than any other place on earth. But I think I'd like to go anywhere, really."

The janitor stared at her again for a moment, smiling awkwardly in a way that only made Mary feel uncomfortable.

"You know," he finally said, "life is always better when seeking adventures."

Boy, did she ever know that. She didn't need the janitor to tell her.

"I wish I could have adventures," she admitted. "But if my father has his way, I'll be here forever. He's not a fan of traveling."

"Well, that's understandable," the janitor replied. "After all, adventures don't come cheaply. And they take time. Maybe it's best to just imagine adventures here in the museum."

Yeah right, she thought. *Easier said than done.*

"That's what Dad always says," Mary replied. "But it's not the same."

Not anymore, she added silently.

"I've been around the world a time or two," the janitor said. "It can be more trouble than it's worth. But maybe things will get better. Perhaps in your lifetime, people will be able to travel wherever and whenever they desire, and in the blink of an eye."

Mary laughed, realizing she'd only just been wishing for the same thing.

"That would be nice," she said. "But with my luck, it still wouldn't work for me."

"I'll tell you this," the janitor said. "Whoever discovers a way to make it happen will become very rich, and powerful."

"Well, maybe I need to start studying harder so I can be the one to discover it," she said.

"Not unless I discover it first," replied the janitor.

A strange greedy look enveloped him, his eyes reflecting like fire in the spotlight. The change in his demeanor caught Mary off guard.

"What do you mean?" she asked.

The janitor shook his head slightly.

"Oh, nothing," he said. "I'm getting old, so I say strange things sometimes. I should probably get back to work. Have a nice night."

Before Mary could respond, he turned away abruptly, and resumed sweeping his way down the dark hallway and out of sight.

Mary wasn't sure what to think about the exchange. There certainly was something strange about that janitor. She shrugged, and turned back to the map.

As soon as she did, her imagination flooded back to life, but only for a few seconds. Voices echoed from somewhere in the museum, jolting Mary's memory and reminding her of the game. Hastily, she tore away from the map, desperately seeking for a place to hide.

It was too late. Before she could even step away, Helen

and Ike emerged into the corridor. Standing below the map's spotlight, Mary had nowhere to go.

"I found you," Ike said sarcastically. "Nice hiding spot."

"Oh man, not again!" Helen said, slapping her palm to her forehead.

"I'm sorry," Mary replied. "It's just that I—"

"We know," Helen said. "You and your map thing."

"It wasn't just that," Mary said. "That old janitor came by and started talking to me, and I couldn't hide until he left."

"Uh-huh, sure," Ike said. "And it's just a coincidence that you're in front of your geek map."

Mary blushed, realizing she was caught.

"Well, so what?" she said in defense. "You can laugh all you want, but if I'm going to start traveling the world soon, I have to be ready. So stop making fun of me, and maybe I'll let you come with me."

Ike and Helen didn't share her enthusiasm. Helen pretended to yawn, as if bored.

"Whatever you say, Magellan," she teased. "If you ever do travel the world, you'll need me there anyway to get your wimpy butt out of trouble whenever you find it. Until then, can we at least have fun while we're stuck here?"

"Who's not having fun?" said a man's voice.

Into the corridor stepped Lewis Tucker, chief curator of

the Charleston World Museum.

"That's impossible," he continued. "A closed museum, all to yourselves? It's the happiest place on earth!"

"I think you're confused with Disneyland, Dad," said Ike.

"We *were* playing hide and seek, but Mary quit on us in the middle of the game," Helen said. "She got lost in one of her map fantasies again."

"Oh she did, did she?" Dad turned to Mary and raised a questioning eyebrow. "What was it this time? The Trans-Siberian railroad? The Australian outback?"

"Dad, I *really* want to go to the Amazon!" she blurted out. "You know my twelfth birthday is coming up next year. Maybe we could make it a family trip?"

"Now hold on there, Mary," Dad interrupted with a laugh. "We've talked about this time and time again. You know how expensive and difficult it is to take a big trip like that."

"I know, but I'll do anything you ask. I can do extra chores for a year, or I could … "

Mary could tell by the smile on his face that he wasn't taking her seriously.

"Dad, if we send Mary to the Amazon, can I have her room?" Ike asked.

"Nobody's going to the Amazon," said Dad. "For crying

out loud, your own father runs one of the biggest museums in all of South Carolina. We can enjoy places without *actually* having to go there."

"But Dad! Please? Will you at least think about it?" Mary begged.

"I'm sorry, my girl," Dad said. "But the only place we're traveling to right now is home for dinner. If we don't get there soon, your mother might banish *me* to the Amazon. Let's not hear any more about this traveling nonsense, okay?"

"Yes, sir," Mary said, deflated.

There had to be some way to convince him. Pestering Dad for months on end to let her travel was clearly not working. "Not until you're older," she was always told. But Mary didn't think she could be that patient. It wouldn't be easy to convince Dad to change his mind, and she knew her dream was a big one. But she was smart enough to find away. Maybe she was just going about all wrong. Maybe if she started smaller …

"If we can't go to the Amazon, could we at least go to Disneyworld?" she asked, flashing her father a big smile.

"Oooohhh, I'd like to second that motion," Ike said, also beaming.

"I volunteer to come as a chaperone," Helen offered.

"Why me?" Dad said, raising both hands into the air

while talking toward the sky.

Mary and Ike laughed as they said goodbye to Helen, who waited as her father, the museum's head of security, locked up the building.

I'll find a way to convince him, Mary told herself as she buckled her seatbelt.

If there was a way, she'd figure it out. After all, she'd never given up on anything before.

CHAPTER TWO

Dinner with Grandpa

"Grandpa's here!" Mary shouted as Dad pulled the car into the driveway.

As they came to a stop, both Mary and Ike stripped off their seat belts and bolted from the vehicle. Mary leapt into the arms of the tall, thin man who stood on her front porch, waiting to embrace her. Grandpa was nearly knocked over backward by Mary's forceful hug.

"Well, hello, it's nice to see you too," Grandpa said, flashing the bright white teeth that lined his ever-wide smile.

He laughed as he tried to keep his balance, then planted a big kiss on Mary's darkly freckled cheek.

"We didn't know you were coming over tonight," Ike exclaimed.

"Well, to tell you the truth, neither did I," admitted Grandpa. "That is to say, at least not until your wonderful mother called me up and invited me over about an hour ago. How could I say no to a real home-cooked meal? It sure beats the canned soup I planned for supper."

Mary looked nervously at Dad, wondering how he'd react to Grandpa's unexpected appearance. Dad's face was blank of any emotion. He didn't say a word, instead walking straight into the house without even greeting his father. Grandpa looked longingly at his son, sadness crossing his face as Dad passed silently by.

"Come on, Grandpa," Mary said, trying to distract him from the moment. "Let's go see what Mom made for dinner."

The tension soon evaporated away as they stood in a home full of the aroma of food cooking. Following the delicious smells, Mary could tell that Mom had gone all out tonight.

"Meat!" Ike exclaimed, sounding carnivorous.

"And Jean's world-famous mashed potatoes," Grandpa added. "Now I'm definitely glad I came over!"

Everybody gathered around the dinner table, anxious to see what else Mom had prepared.

"I want to sit next to him!" Ike complained as Mary tried to take the seat next to Grandpa.

"You know, one of you could sit on either side," Mom

suggested as she stepped into the room.

Soon they were all seated, with a meal in front of them that was large enough to feed a small army. In addition to the steak and potatoes, there was hot-steamed broccoli dripping with melted butter, and flaky, freshly-baked dinner rolls. Mary felt her stomach rumble in anticipation.

Ike, with his customarily bad manners, starting shoveling food onto his own plate, ignoring everyone else. Mary made sure that Grandpa got some of everything, and shot a disapproving look at her brother.

Ike didn't notice, as he was intently focused on building what looked like a volcano out of his mashed potatoes. He looked up at her, opening his eyes wide and smiling like a mad scientist.

"Behold my creation!" he said.

Before Mary could blink, Ike violently threw his face into the mashed potato volcano and started eating, straight from the plate, with no hands. He made noises like a wild animal.

"Excuse me, mister? Did you forget that we have a strict no-feral-child policy at the dinner table?" Mom scolded.

Ike looked up, not saying anything, but with mashed potatoes smeared across the lens of his glasses. He tried to bite Mom's finger as she wagged it at him from across the table.

"I always thought he might be part snapping turtle," Grandpa said, earning laughs from everybody, except Dad.

"So, Jean, what's the special occasion?" asked Dad, finally breaking his silence.

"No special occasion," Mom replied casually. "I just realized we aren't spending as much quality time together as a family. Everybody's always so busy with school and work. But isn't this what normal families do? Sit and eat together, having normal conversations?"

"A great suggestion, Jean," Grandpa agreed. "And why don't I start some of that normal conversation? I'd been hoping these young folks would let an old man know what's going on in the school these days."

"It's still standing." Ike said quickly. "It hasn't burnt down yet."

A piece of steak fell from Ike's fork before it could reach his mouth, bouncing off his wrinkled school uniform and leaving a brownish grease stain. Mom groaned as she leaned across the table and started rubbing at the stain with a wet napkin.

"Well, that's a good thing, isn't it?" Grandpa asked.

"Only if you're Mary," Ike replied.

"Mrs. Lehmann has been teaching us about the conservation of trees," Mary piped in, hoping to spare them all from more of Ike's attempted humor.

"Oh, now that sounds interesting," said Mom, clearly eager to do the same. "And what have you learned so far, dear?"

"That too many trees are being cut down, and that more and more forests are being destroyed every year," Mary answered in a depressed tone.

She paused for dramatic effect.

"Especially in the rainforest."

Dad coughed, almost choking on a piece of broccoli.

"You know Grandpa, Mary's an expert on the rainforest," Ike jumped in. "In fact, she's taking us all there for her birthday."

Mary ignored her brother and kept talking.

"Mrs. Lehmann said that one of the biggest reasons the trees are destroyed is so people can raise cows. They burn down the trees in areas and turn the land into fields. Then, they sell the cows for beef in other countries."

Mary looked questioningly down at the steak on her plate.

"Really?" said Mom, also glancing at her own plate. "I had no idea. Do you think these steaks came from cows raised in the rainforest?"

"I hope not," Mary said. "Because when the cows graze

in the areas where the forest used to be, they ruin the soil so the trees won't ever grow back. It's destroying the rainforest."

"Yeah, because of too many cow pies," Ike inserted.

"Ike!" Mom reprimanded, though she was trying to hold back her own laughter.

It annoyed Mary that this was turning into a joke.

"Don't worry too much, Mary," Dad said, noticing her frown. "A lot of smart people are working hard to protect the rainforests. It's a big place and a lot of the land's preserved. It won't all be destroyed."

"I know," Mary said. "But it still isn't good that so much of it keeps getting burned or cut down. It makes me sad to think about all the animals that have their natural habitats destroyed. Mrs. Lehmann said that thousands of different species go extinct every year. She said that some of them are animals we don't even know about yet."

"That's really a shame," Mom said, now sounding genuinely concerned. "I wonder if there's anything we could do?"

"Maybe we should eat more cow pies?" Ike suggested.

This time not even Mom laughed.

"Remember what I said about jokes only being funny the first time?" she asked.

Ike sat back and pouted at his failed attempt at humor.

Somehow he now had bits of broccoli stuck in his dark hair.

"One of the things we talked about was doing research to make sure that our beef doesn't come from cows raised in areas cleared from the rainforests. It's at least one thing we could do." Mary suggested.

"Yes!" Mom said, brightening. "I think that's a great idea. I'll do some research on the internet and find out which companies are okay to use."

"I'm proud of you Mary," Grandpa said, giving her a pat on the shoulder. "You're a wise girl for your age. We need more people like you who want to make the world a better place."

Mary beamed. Being praised by her beloved grandfather felt as good as anything she could imagine.

Grandpa sat back with a thoughtful look on his face. He seemed to be contemplating something pleasant.

"The rainforests really are so beautiful, and so full of life. They were always one my favorite places to visit," he said, to nobody in particular.

Suddenly, Grandpa seemed to realize what he was saying, and snapped back to reality.

"Anyway, that's not important. What else have you kids been doing in school?"

Mary, shocked, completely ignored his question.

"Grandpa, you've *been* to the Amazon before?" she asked.

"Well … " he said, carefully, " … yes, but it was all such a long time ago. I don't really remember that much."

Mary knew he wasn't telling the whole truth. Grandpa nervously glanced over at Dad as he spoke. Dad refused to look up, instead remaining focused on his food.

"Tell me about it, please?" Mary pleaded. "I want to go to the rainforest more than anything. What was it like? What did you see? Did you see any animals? Did you—"

"Why don't we talk about something else?" Dad said. "Your grandfather doesn't want to be bombarded with all these questions."

Mary winced. She'd pushed too far again.

"Maybe your father's right," Grandpa said. "We can talk about it another time."

"Oh Lewis, don't be that way," Mom cut in. "I want to hear about it too. Especially after what Mary's been telling us about the rainforest, it might be nice to hear from somebody who's actually been there before."

"Jean, I really don't think that's a good idea," Dad said, trying to gesture at Mary with his eyeballs.

Mom either didn't notice or ignored Dad's nonverbal pleas.

"Go on, Ephraim," Mom said. "Tell us about it."

"Well, I'll try to tell you what I remember, but like I said, it was a long time ago. When you get old, your memory starts to fade, you know," Grandpa said, still proceeding with obvious caution.

Dad looked particularly annoyed, but instead of saying anything, went back to concentrating on his food.

Mary sat attentively and faced her grandfather.

"Tell me everything," she demanded.

"Well, I remember it being very loud for one thing." Grandpa said. "There were animals everywhere making some sort of noise. Birds, monkeys, insects. Oh, and it's also extremely hot and humid. Even the humidity here in the South is nothing compared to the rainforest. I was constantly sweating."

"Why did you go there? What did you do? How—"

"Mary!" Dad was now clearly angry. "I thought I made myself clear! I don't want to hear any more talk about the rainforest, or about traveling, or about anything else!"

Mary immediately went very quiet and sank into her chair. She felt tears well up in her eyes.

"Lewis, what's wrong?" Mom asked, genuinely surprised at Dad's outburst.

"It's nothing," Dad said sharply. "But if you'll excuse me, I have some work to do."

Before anybody could say another word, Dad stood up from the table, and stormed out of the room. Nobody said a thing, clearly shocked at his eruption. Dad often got annoyed, but was rarely angry like that.

Grandpa cast another sad look at Dad as he left the room. Mary wished she knew why there was always this wall between them. What had happened?

Later that night, lying in her bed, Mary couldn't stop thinking about the incident. She couldn't understand why Dad was so opposed to traveling. Mary knew that a trip to the rainforest was a longshot, but what hurt the most was that Dad wasn't even willing to talk to her about it. It was her dream, and it was as if he was trying to crush it before it could even grow.

A knock sounded on her bedroom door.

"Mary, may I come in?" Dad's voice called from the other side.

"I guess," Mary said, coldly.

Dad entered and sat at the foot of her bed.

"Mary, I'm sorry for the way I reacted at supper this evening," he apologized. "It was wrong of me to get angry like that. I know that you really want to travel and see the world."

Mary sat up in her bed.

"Dad, I know I can do it!" she blurted out, hoping this

would be her chance. "Believe me, I'll do all the research necessary. Don't worry, it'll be safe."

"Mary, I'm sorry, but it is a little bit more complicated than that," Dad said. "First of all, you're only eleven. But there's something more than that. It's hard for me to explain. I'm just … I'm just afraid of what might happen."

"Is it the money? I promise I'll do whatever I can to earn it," she reasoned.

"No, it's not that," he said, staring at the wall. "I just can't, I mean, it would be too hard … "

"What is it?" Mary asked, eager to hear whatever was so hard for him to say.

"I'll tell you about it someday. The subject's just still a little too sensitive for me," he confessed, his voice quivering slightly.

Dad stood up and walked toward the door. Mary thought she saw the glisten of tears in his eyes.

"You're a wonderful girl, Mary," he said. "I love you. Keep working hard, and I'm sure you'll find all the adventure you'll ever need."

"So does that mean you'll still think about us going on a trip together?" Mary asked, hopeful.

Dad sighed.

"We'll see, Mary. We'll see."

He walked into the corridor, and shut the door.

CHAPTER THREE

The Mysterious Trunk

For the next two weeks, Mary was extra helpful around the house. She worked harder than ever at school. She knew that Dad hadn't *actually* agreed to let her take a trip, but she had to at least try to win him over. He couldn't hold out forever, could he?

Every time Dad praised Mary for her efforts, she gently hinted that she hoped it was enough to convince him to let her travel. She was careful, not wanting to push too hard and undo all of her hard work. Yet every time she tried, Dad quickly changed the subject.

"I don't know what else I can do!" Mary lamented to Ike and Helen, as the three children sat bored in the museum one afternoon.

"Maybe we could play hide and seek?" Ike suggested.

"No way," Helen protested. "There's nowhere new to hide."

"I'm not talking about that," Mary said. "I'm talking about convincing Dad to let me travel."

"I hate to break it to you, Mary," said Helen. "But fifth-graders don't travel the world. You might have to wait until you're old enough to go on your own, just like everybody else."

"I'm pretty sure Mary's already, like, forty," Ike joked.

"I really hope you're wrong, Helen," said Mary in despair. "I don't think I can wait that long. I want to go now!"

"Come on," Helen said, standing up. "Let's find something else to take your mind off traveling. If you really want to be an explorer, so why not start smaller, like with the warehouse?"

Helen raised an eyebrow, shooting Mary a devious look.

Mary couldn't help but laugh. Helen always had a way of distracting her from whatever was on her mind. Sometimes that was a bad thing, but right now, Mary welcomed the chance to put her depression aside.

"Why not?" Mary said, jumping up and following Helen.

The museum's warehouse was located in an enormous open area below the ground floor. The entire space was filled with stacked crates, which contained the museum's collection of items currently not on display. Going into the warehouse was technically off limits, but Mary knew they'd stay out of any real trouble. Besides, it would still be another couple of hours before Dad was ready to go.

"Isn't it a little bit dark in there?" Ike asked, trying not to sound afraid. "You know, I just don't want to have to save you girls if you think you see a ghost or something."

"Oh sure," Helen said. "We'll definitely need the brave little nine-year-old to keep us safe. Oh, Ike, my hero!"

Mary and Helen both got a good laugh at Ike's expense. He shrugged off their teasing.

"I'm just saying," he said. "Girls are afraid of the dark sometimes."

"Ike, if you're scared, you don't have to go down there with us," Mary said.

"I'm not scared!" Ike insisted as he followed them toward the stairway that led to the warehouse.

It got progressively darker as they descended the long staircase. Soon, there was barely enough light to see the steps in front of them. Once they reached the basement floor, Helen quickly punched in a few numbers on the keypad, disabling the warehouse's alarm system.

"Now, where's that light switch?" Ike asked, looking for

the nearby master control for the overhead lighting.

"I don't think so," Mary said, giving Helen a knowing nudge. "The whole idea is that we need to be explorers in the dark."

"Yeah, that's right," Helen said, catching Mary's clue. "And in this game we're not allowed to speak to each other either. The first one who makes it through the maze of crates and reaches the loading dock on the other side is the winner."

"In the … dark?" Ike asked, timidly. "Don't you think that'll be a little bit too hard?"

"Of course," Mary replied. "But that's why it's fun. You said you weren't afraid, right?"

Helen's game actually did sound fun. Helen would win, of course. She always won at these types of games. But it was at least something new and different.

"Fine," Ike relented. "I just wanted to make sure that you're all okay with being in the dark."

"Everybody ready?" Mary asked.

"Ready," Helen said.

"I guess so," Ike said.

"On your marks … get set … GO!"

They plunged into the dark room, each taking a different path and feeling their way through the maze of crates.

Mary moved deeper and deeper into the darkness. There

were so many crates! Dad said that at any given time, only about five percent of the museum's collection was actually on display. Some items were on loan to other museums, but the vast majority of what the museum owned was jammed into this warehouse. Mary wondered how they'd ever acquired so much.

As she maneuvered through the wooden labyrinth, Mary nearly tripped over a long, flat crate in her path. She carefully stepped over it. On the other side, to her dismay, Mary found a dead end, a wall of stacked crates blocking her path. How was she supposed to get through now?

Mary bent down, hoping to find another way through. Much to her delight, she discovered a small open space between two crates. It was just large enough to let her squeeze through. It could be a shortcut, which meant she might be able to beat Helen after all.

As she crawled on her hands and knees, Mary heard Ike fumbling his way through the warehouse. She stifled a giggle as he crashed into some crates.

"For the love of barnacles!" he yelled in frustration.

Mary continued to squeeze forward through the tiny tunnel, which continued for several feet. She hoped she'd find the other side soon.

Her luck ran out. Instead of leading to an exit, Mary

found her way completely blocked by another crate. She tried in vain to find a way around it.

As she explored with her hands, she noticed something strange. This crate wasn't made of plywood like the others. Instead, it was made of some other sort of hard, smooth material with metallic edges. On the side of the crate, Mary felt a large, flat metal disk with a keyhole in its center.

What was this thing, and why was it buried here under all these crates?

Without warning, the lights came on in the warehouse, shining through spaces in the boxes above her. Mary gulped, fearing that Dad had discovered them.

"What did you do that for?" Helen yelled from the far end of the warehouse.

"Come on, it's impossible to see anything in this place in the dark!" Ike yelled back.

Mary sighed in relief, thankful that Dad hadn't walked in on them after all.

Before Mary could slide backward out of the tunnel, she caught a glimpse of the odd crate that had blocked her way. With the lights now on, Mary could just make out some of its details. It wasn't a crate after all, but another box which had previously been inside one of the normal plywood crates. Somehow, the crate's side had broken open, revealing the strange box it contained. Something about it looked vaguely familiar to Mary. It took her a minute to realize what it was. As soon as she did, she was instantly filled with excitement.

An old-fashioned travel trunk! It was well worn, and the edges were lined with tarnished and dented metal. The exposed side of the trunk had a handle, two metal buckles, and several faded labels, which said "FRAGILE" or "HANDLE WITH CARE." Mary had no idea why this well-used suitcase of a seasoned traveler would be among the museum's collection. It certainly wasn't like any of the other items the museum tended to display. Mary's mind fantasized about all the distant lands this old box had likely seen. She was jealous that a simple suitcase had probably been all over the world, while she hadn't been anywhere.

It was cramped in the tunnel under the crates, and Mary wanted to get a better look at the travel trunk. Straining, she grabbed the case's handle and pulled the heavy trunk as she backed out of the tunnel. It was hard to maneuver in the tight space, but fortunately, there was just enough room to slide the trunk out into the open light.

When she emerged from the tunnel, the first thing Mary noticed was a small brass nameplate with an inscription: "PROPERTY OF E. B. TUCKER"

Mary's eyes almost popped out of her skull when she

realized what she was seeing. She knew that name all too well.

"Ike, Helen, come over here and look at this!" Mary yelled in exhilaration.

Within a few moments they were at her side, peering down at Mary's discovery.

"What is it?" Helen asked.

"It's an old travel trunk," Mary answered reverently. "One that's probably been used to travel around the world."

"Seriously, Mary?" Ike complained. "You think we're going to get as excited as you over an old suitcase?"

"You will when you see this."

Mary triumphantly pointed to the inscription.

"What are you talking about—" Ike said, stopping short as he read the label.

His mouth and eyes both opened wide.

"It's Grandpa's!" he exclaimed. "E. B. Tucker is Ephraim Byron Tucker! But how did it get here?"

"Well, Grandpa did work here for years," Mary said. "But this looks more like his personal property. I have no idea why he'd put it here in the warehouse."

"I wish we could see what's inside," Ike said.

"Then why don't you open it, genius?" Helen suggested.

Mary and Ike looked at each other for a moment, as if unsure whether they actually should do it.

"Well," said Ike, "If this is Grandpa's personal suitcase, wouldn't he show us what's inside anyway if he were here?"

The logic was enough to convince Mary. Both she and Ike simultaneously dove toward the trunk and started unfastening its metal buckles.

Once the buckles were unfastened, they tried to push open the lid. It wouldn't budge. Mary had forgotten about the keyhole. Indeed, as she found the metal disc, she discovered that a big, locking clasp held the lid firmly closed. Mary sighed with dashed hopes.

"We can't open it without the key," Ike complained.

"I guess we'll have to ask Grandpa about it next time we see him," Mary said. "Just make sure it is not when Dad's around."

"Step aside, amateurs," Helen said, pushing past them and toward the travel trunk. "Keys are completely overrated."

Helen hunched over and fumbled around with the locked clasp for a minute. She forcefully made a pushing motion, and a metallic "pop" sounded. Helen, holding a small screwdriver in her hand, stood up to reveal the previously locked clasp, now opened wide. She spun the tool around her finger, and blew on it like a smoking pistol.

"You're welcome," she said.

"Wait a minute," Mary said, confused. "How did you—"

"Oh please," Helen said. "Old locks like this are hard to pick, but they're not very strong. My parents still have one similar to this on our back gate. When I was seven, they gave me a key one day when I was coming home from school early. They told me it was mine, and not to lose it. Well, I lost it three days later. I was too afraid to tell them, but I learned fast enough that with the right leverage, you can pop these clasps right open."

Mary stared at Helen, dumbfounded. Her friend was always full of surprises. But before she could think any more about Helen's unexpected skill set, Mary remembered the trunk, which now sat unlocked before her. She reached down, and slowly lifted the lid.

CHAPTER FOUR

A Globe of Glass

"Now that's what I'm talking about!" Ike said as he pulled a long, shiny blade from the trunk.

It looked like a sword, only not as long, and with a much wider blade. Ike held it high above his head as he yelled like a gladiator calling out to an invisible opponent.

"Come on and fight like a man!"

"Oh, put it away, Ike," Helen said. "I don't even trust you with plastic scissors, and I'd like to keep my eyeballs today."

Ike responded with his best ninja impression. Pushing his glasses up his nose, he swung the blade around, adding his own kung-fu sound effects. It didn't look natural with his stocky body, short legs, and thick mushroom of hair. Mary ignored her brother, but looked at the sword. She knew it wasn't really a sword, but rather a machete—a long, wide knife that was used to cut through dense jungles.

It would be perfect for the rainforest, Mary thought, wondering whether Grandpa had used the machete during his trips to the Amazon.

Mary turned back to the open trunk to see what else it contained. She pulled out a pair of army green backpacks made from a thick, canvas-like material. She opened one of them, and inside found a small leather-bound book, some folded raincoats, and two metal canteens, and a few other things. Without thinking, Mary replaced the items and slung the backpack over her shoulders as she continued to dig through the trunk. Every item caused Mary to wonder how each had been used in adventures around the world.

As she rummaged deeper, Mary's fingers made contact with the edge of a smaller box, buried beneath the assortment of gear. It was a sturdy, cubical case of smooth metal. Mary tried to lift it, but found it was too heavy. Increasingly curious, she cleared the items covering the metal box until its entire lid was exposed. Mary unlatched the lid, and opened the case.

She was confused by what she found. Instead of a fancy camera or some other piece of valuable equipment, Mary found a small, simple-looking instrument. It was unlike anything she'd ever seen, and she didn't have the slightest clue what it was.

The most striking part of the unknown object was a smooth sphere of pale glass, about the size of a large orange. The sphere was mounted on a golden stand, and tilted at an angle.

Mary carefully lifted the strange, heavy artifact out of its case.

"Look at this weird glass ball," she said. "It's like a globe, only without a map."

"Maybe it's a globe of the moon?" Ike suggested, stopping his machete swinging to come and admire Mary's find.

"What do you think it does?" Helen asked.

"Beats me," Mary replied, honestly.

She turned the globe-like item around a few times, searching for anything that might reveal its purpose. Why would a useless object be kept in such a secure, padded case? And what was it doing in Grandpa's old travel trunk anyway?

Mary touched the surface of the glass sphere, and found that it could spin just like a regular globe. The thick glass rotated effortlessly as Mary gave it a push with her fingers.

The glass orb swiveled normally a few times when, without warning, it began rotating rapidly. It was like it had a mind of its own!

The rotations grew faster and faster, and within seconds,

the ball of glass was spinning on its stand at top speed. As the globe continue to whirl, the pale glass suddenly lit up.

Mary was so startled she almost dropped it.

"Holy cow!" Ike yelled, jumping back. "What is it?"

"It *is* a globe!" Mary said, once she'd recovered from her shock.

The light of the orb steadily grew brighter, revealing a map of the world where, a moment earlier, there'd only been blank, pale glass. Though the glass was still spinning, the illuminated image of the earth's surface didn't move.

The map didn't look exactly like those found on other globes. It showed no borders of countries, nor did any names of places appear. Mary realized that it looked much like pictures she'd seen of the earth as taken from space, with deep blue oceans and green and brownish land masses. Even white clouds were visible, covering parts of the planet's surface. It was amazing!

"The clouds are moving," Helen noted in surprise.

Mary couldn't figure out how such a small object could project a map of the world in such intricate detail. She watched the clouds slowly drift over the map, gradually changing their shape. Gazing deeper into the glass, more details came into focus. Mary could see the rippling movements of the ocean and slow currents churning deep within the water.

"This is the most unbelievable thing I've ever seen," Mary exclaimed in sheer awe.

Mary turned the globe in her hands, searching again for any indicator of how it worked. As she tipped it upward, Mary was treated to a great view of South America.

"Look at this," she said. "It's the Amazon."

Sure enough, by gazing deep into the globe, Mary distinctly saw a pattern of brownish lines branching like tiny veins through the heart of South America, indicating the mighty river.

"Wow, Mary," said Ike. "I think you broke your record. Seven minutes without mentioning the Amazon. Way to go!"

Mary ignored Ike and fixated on the Amazon. It looked far more beautiful than it did on conventional maps. The rainforest was a deep green, greener than any other part of the globe.

Deep within her, Mary felt a funny sensation. An energy came from the spinning sphere, which called out to her in a silent yet powerful voice.

Touch the globe, she heard in her mind.

Mary slowly moved her finger closer to the glass surface. She felt a surge of nervous anticipation. She could feel that something exciting was about to happen. Looking over at Ike and Helen, Mary saw that they both felt the sensation too.

Was it a good excitement, or were her instincts warning her of danger?

It didn't matter. Mary's urge to touch the globe was too strong. Her finger made contact with the spinning glass, right in the heart of the Amazon. Just as she did, Helen reached out with a gasp and clasped Mary by the arm.

"Don't touch it!" she said, but too late.

In the blink of an eye, something extraordinary happened. The globe grew! Mary wasn't sure if the globe was actually changing in size, but her view of it certainly did. Within a few seconds, the warehouse completely disappeared, and all she could see was a giant earth before her. Mary glanced to one side, to see a frightened Helen. Her iron grip on Mary's arm felt like a vice. Mary looked to the other side for Ike, but he was nowhere to be found.

"Mary?" Helen said nervously. "What's happening?"

Mary returned her gaze to the massive globe in front of her. She felt like she was floating in outer space, looking down at the surface of the planet. Mary could still feel the globe in her hand and her finger pressed against the glass, even though the globe had disappeared. Steadily, the earth continued to grow larger. She and Helen were actually zooming in toward the point where Mary's finger made contact.

Helen shrieked as she felt them moving, and suddenly let

go of Mary's arm.

"Helen!" Mary cried, watching her friend vanished completely into thin air.

Shocked by the turn of events, Mary quickly pulled her finger away from the glass. Her expanded view of the world faded, and the globe returned to its original size, once again visible in her hand.

"What just happened?" Mary asked with a trembling voice.

She turned to Ike, who looked like he was about to throw up.

"You tell me," he said. "You both dis … you disappeared completely!"

"What?" Mary said. "You couldn't see us either?"

Ike shook his head.

"No," he said. "Helen came back first, then you."

"That thing is freaky," Helen said, clearly disturbed. "It was like we were in a life size version of Google Earth! It felt like we were falling from space."

"What?" said Ike, suddenly not looking quite so woozy. "That sounds awesome! I want to see what it does!"

Mary wasn't sure what to say. What exactly could this little globe do? Her heart was pounding, but despite the feelings of anxiety, the almost irresistible urge to touch the globe returned.

"Okay Ike, hold on to me and I'll touch it again," she said.

"Just don't let go. When Helen let go of me, she disappeared."

"Mary," Helen said quietly, while squeezing Mary's shoulder. "Are you sure this is a good idea? I have a really funny feeling about this. I don't think I've ever been more scared in my life."

"On second thought," Ike said, letting go of Mary, "maybe Helen's right. Maybe there's a reason Grandpa kept this thing hidden here."

"Don't worry," Mary assured them. "Last time everything went back to normal the second I pulled my finger away from the glass. I came right back to the warehouse, and so did Helen when she let go."

Mary looked at Helen and Ike. She was sure they were curious too. Finally, Helen gave Mary a reluctant nod. She and Ike each put a hand on Mary's shoulder, and Mary reached her finger toward the spinning glass once again.

"My goodness, you've found it!" said a deep voice from somewhere behind them.

Mary turned in surprise to see who had spoken. It was the old janitor. How had he been able to sneak up on her once again? Mary stared at him in confusion, her finger hovered a centimeter away from the glass.

"I've been looking for this for forty years, and here it is!" he exclaimed, gleefully, reaching out and taking a step toward Mary. "Hurry, Child, hand it over!"

CHAPTER FIVE

Nowhere to Run

Mary was trapped. She, Ike, and Helen were backed against a wall of crates, and the old janitor was closing in.

"Don't be afraid, just give me my globe," he said, with insatiable greed in his eyes.

Instinctively, Mary clutched the still-spinning globe tightly against her chest. She tried to another step backward, but the wall prevented that. There was nowhere to run.

"It doesn't belong to you," Mary said, trembling in fear as the janitor loomed nearer. "It was in my grandfather's travel case."

"Don't be foolish, child," the man snapped back. "It's

mine, and nothing will stop me from finally getting it!"

Mary let out a small scream of panic when he reached into his jacket pocket and extracted a black handgun. He aimed it directly at her. Mary had been afraid already. Now she was terrified.

"Now, be a good girl and give me the globe. Hand it over without any trouble, and I promise that nobody will get hurt," said the old man.

He didn't sound very convincing.

A thousand thoughts raced through Mary's mind. Her heart was pounding out of control. What could she do? She was petrified with a fear she'd never felt before, but at the same time, she knew that she could *not*, under any circumstance, allow this man to get the globe.

"What are you waiting for?" Ike whispered urgently. "Just give it to him already!"

Mary was still frozen. There had to be something she could do.

Touch the globe. The powerful, penetrating thought came to her mind, just as it had before.

But would that work? When she touched it the first time, Ike said they disappeared. Would they be able to escape the janitor?

Touch the globe! came the urge once again.

With the old man's pistol still trained on her, Mary glanced down nervously at the globe. Her hands were shaking uncontrollably, and she could barely even hold on to the heavy object.

Here goes nothing, she thought, as she reached out with a quivering finger.

Before she could change her mind, Mary pressed against the surface of the spinning glass.

"Wait, stop!" the man yelled, dropping his gun and lunging at them. "Don't touch it!"

His hand was inches away from the globe as he faded into nothing. As before, the room was gone, replaced by the enormous view of the earth below.

Mary braced herself, half expecting to still feel the janitor wrench the globe from her fingers at any moment, invisible or not. But to her great relief, he was gone.

"It worked," she whispered.

"What's happening?" Ike said, fear and surprise heavy in his voice.

"I touched the globe," Mary said. "Whatever you do, don't let go of me, or you'll end up back in the warehouse."

Mary felt both Ike and Helen immediately tighten their grips on her shoulder.

Everybody was silent, and for a moment, all Mary could

hear was the sound of three pounding heartbeats. Below, the dazzling earth shone like a giant blue orb. Mary kept her finger held firmly against the invisible glass, and the earth continued to grow.

"So what are we gonna do?" Helen finally asked. "Just hang out here in space forever?"

"I don't know," Mary answered, truthfully. "But I can't let go now."

"Won't we have to go back at some point?" Ike asked.

"I'd rather be floating out here in fake outer space than in that warehouse with a gun pointed at me," said Mary. "Maybe if we stay out here long enough, the old man will eventually leave."

"I don't know," said Ike. "He looked pretty serious about wanting the globe. What if he just sits there and waits for us to reappear?"

"Eventually he'll have to leave," Helen said. "My dad will come looking for us, and when he doesn't find us, the first thing he'll do is check the security cameras. He'll see everything that happened, and I doubt the janitor will want to wait around to deal with him."

Ike seemed satisfied by the answer, and Mary suggested they stay at least three hours, just to be sure.

"Fine by me," Ike agreed. "Like you said, better out here

then back there with the crazy guy."

Throughout their conversation, Mary watched as the massive earth grew before them. She could still feel the globe, now held more tightly in her hands than ever. She pressed as hard as she could, not daring to take her finger off the glass.

Exploring the amazing view before her, Mary's fear from being held at gunpoint slowly dissolved. Her heart rate slowed, and her thoughts instead turned to the exhilarating experience of zooming in toward this indescribably beautiful view. It was far more vivid than any of her imagined adventures had ever been.

Staying out here for a few hours won't be that bad at all, she thought.

Secretly, Mary suspected she could stay out there for much longer if she wanted to. The wall map in the museum that she so dearly loved seemed small and dull compared to the magnificent view before her now.

Still, Mary was troubled by the fact that she didn't know how this globe worked. Question after question raced through her mind as she tried to puzzle out the remarkable object. Was it connected to a satellite or telescope? How close would they zoom in if she kept pressing?

"How close to the earth do you think this will take us?" asked Helen, as if reading Mary's mind.

"I don't know," Mary answered. "But since we have time, why don't we find out?"

Mary wasn't paying attention to where she pointed at first, but almost subconsciously, began guiding their descent in the direction of the Amazon. As the world got bigger, Mary periodically made slight adjustments by sliding her finger along the glass. She did this instinctively, and it worked. As her finger moved, so did the center of their descent.

The Amazon steadily grew more visible. Its thousands of arms branched through the rainforest. They were now so close that Mary could no longer see the Atlantic or Pacific Oceans to either side of South America. All she saw was a giant mass of green, stretching as far as her eyes could see. Though no borders nor labels were visible, Mary guessed they were approaching somewhere near the point where Brazil, Colombia, and Peru all met.

As they zoomed in even closer, more details became clear. Mary could plainly make out the tops of thousands of trees, all bunched up together to create a solid, vast canopy of leaves.

"Birds!" Ike yelled.

Mary looked, and saw a colorful flock flying far below. They were tiny from this distance, but there was no mistaking those striking blues, reds, and golds.

"They're macaws," Mary said, amazed. "And we can actually see them flying. I wonder if we're really looking at what's happening in this part of the world right now?"

Eventually, their descent slowed down. Despite the wonder of the experience, Mary couldn't help but feel a little disappointed that she couldn't get even closer. She wanted the experience of actually being in the Amazon.

Still, they hadn't stopped yet, so Mary kept pressing her finger firmly against the glass, hoping that there would still be more to see.

Ike, from behind, fidgeted and shifted in an attempt to get a better view.

"Be careful!" Mary warned. "What if you accidentally let go?"

"Sorry," Ike said. "I'm just trying to see better."

"Try now," Mary said, lifting her elbow.

Ike adjusted his position, attempting to look under Mary's raised arm. As he did, he smacked his head squarely against her elbow. The jolt caused Mary's finger to slide far along the glass. Their position shifted rapidly, with green trees flying by beneath them. Mary couldn't tell where they were, and the land turned to a green blur. She steadied her finger, trying to get their view of the Amazon back into focus.

"What's wrong with you?" Mary yelled, as their shifting

slowed and trees took shape once again.

The river was now nowhere to be seen.

"Let go, Mary!" Ike pleaded suddenly. "Please! Something isn't right."

"What are you talking about? Everything was fine until you ... "

Mary's words trailed off as the picture came back into full focus. During the confusion of the shifting map, she hadn't realized how close they'd gotten. The trees were right below them. If this were real, her feet would almost be touching the leaves.

And to Mary's surprise, they did.

Her shoes brushed against the top of the canopy. The moment they made contact, everything changed. In an instant, Mary could no longer feel the glass against her finger, nor the floor beneath her feet.

Instead, Mary felt different sensations. Falling. Leaves and branches scraping against her body as she tumbled into a very real tree.

Ike and Helen were screaming, but Mary could hardly hear them over her own cries of fear. She bounced like a pinball between branches as she fell. A moment later, it all stopped as her head hit hard against a branch, and everything went dark.

CHAPTER SIX

How Did We Get Here?

Mary groaned as she tried to open her eyes. Her head throbbed with pain.

"Leave me alone!" she moaned, her eyes refusing to fully open. "Just let me sleep."

Whoever was trying to wake her needed to stop. In her groggy delirium, she wondered who had such tiny hands.

Her tormentor was persistent, brushing Mary's cheek. Whoever it was felt warm and ... hairy? That was strange. It was enough for Mary to finally force open her heavy eyelids.

She felt so dizzy! Blurry lights and shadows flashed before her. Everything looked green. Someone hovered directly above her hazy line of vision. She tried to focus.

"Mom?" Mary asked. "Is that you? What happened? Why's it so loud? Why's everything green?"

Mary felt so confused, and she needed answers. But Mom didn't reply to any of the questions. She simply stood there, silently watching. As Mary's focus cleared, the details of Mom's face finally came into view.

Mary screamed, and Mom hurriedly jumped away.

Only it wasn't Mom. It wasn't even another person! With a jolt, Mary snapped wide awake, the grogginess she felt immediately evaporating.

A monkey?

Mary screamed again, and the gray little monkey, with its black mask-patterned face, moved even further away. When it had moved far enough away, the monkey turned to her and bared its teeth.

Mary sat up quickly, frightened yet anxious to know where she was. She clearly wasn't in her bedroom.

As soon as Mary was upright, her whole body lost its balance and started falling into thin air. She cried out, and instinctively flailed her outstretched arms, hoping to grab onto anything.

Luckily, her hand caught hold of a branch. Mary held on with all of her might as she regained her balance. Nearby, several of the little monkeys congregated, chattering loudly.

She was in a tree! How could that be possible?

Sure enough, as Mary scanned her immediate surroundings, she saw nothing but branches and leaves in every direction.

This wasn't one of her imagined adventures. As real as her imagination had been able to make things feel, it paled in comparison to what she was experiencing now.

With a sudden surge of vertigo, Mary realized what it meant. This was no imagined tree, and she was truly somewhere high above the ground. She'd climbed plenty of trees before, and didn't think she was afraid of heights. But her stomach told her otherwise. Judging by what she could see, this tree was much bigger than any she'd ever climbed before. She braced herself and slowly looked down, searching for the ground. The thick leaves made it nearly impossible to see, but Mary found a small gap, just wide enough to give her a glimpse of the ground below.

Mary's fears were confirmed when she saw that she was more than one hundred feet above the ground. Dizziness surged through her, and she clung to the nearest branch for dear life. She was most definitely afraid of heights after all. Squeezing her eyes shut, Mary tried to push out all thoughts of plummeting to the ground.

Her head was ringing. She tried to focus, and figure out

how she had ended up in such an enormous tree. It was impossible for her to climb this high. Panic set in and her thoughts were a jumble. Yet amidst all the confusion, a voice echoed in her mind.

"Let go, Mary!"

Ike's voice. He'd been yelling at her to let go of something. But what?

With a flash of recognition, it all came back. Mary recalled the old travel case and the globe. She remembered touching the globe in an attempt to escape from the old janitor.

"Oh, no," she gasped in disbelief.

Impossible as it seemed, the globe had brought her *to* the rainforest. What other explanation could there be?

"Let go, Mary!" Ike's voice echoed again in her spinning head.

Ike and Helen! With horror, Mary remembered that they'd been with her when she fell. But where were they now?

As her imagination raced with horrible thoughts of what might have happened to them, it became too much for Mary to bear. She began to cry uncontrollably. She clung to the nearest branch, terrified of falling, with tears streaming down her cheeks. She choked out sobs as she battled awful thoughts of having killed her little brother and her best friend. It was all her fault!

"Helen! Ike!" Mary called out, hoping for a miracle.

It didn't do much good. Her voice was weak with fear, and the noise of rainforest drowned out what little sound she managed. She swallowed and tried again, calling out for Helen and Ike repeatedly. Her voice grew steadily louder, and soon she was yelling their names at the top of her lungs. Her yelling excited the troop of monkeys, who jabbered loudly and swung from branch to branch.

"Mary?"

A soft voice called to her from somewhere up above. Mary stopped yelling and strained to listen through the din of the canopy.

"Mary?"

It was just loud enough for her to make out the voice.

"Ike!" she cried back. "I'm here."

A surge of relief flooded through her as she realized that her brother was alive.

"What happened?" he called back. "Where are we?"

"Hold on," Mary yelled in reply. "Keep talking, and I'll find you."

Mary knew she'd need to loosen her grip on the branch and climb. Even the thought made her throbbing head pound harder. But she didn't have a choice. Taking a deep breath, Mary stood, her feet wobbling on the branch. It took all of her concentration to not think about the long way down.

At first she moved at a snail's pace, deliberately testing each branch to ensure it would support her weight. The tree and its branches were strong, but being cautious was the only thing that gave her enough courage to keep climbing.

It was more physically challenging than she imagined, and sweat poured down her face in the stifling humidity. Mary wiped her eyes as she peered through the leaves above her, hoping to see some sign of Ike.

Finally, she spied a pair of tennis shoes dangling through the branches.

"I see you!" she cried out.

A moment later, panting from the challenging climb, she came face to face with her little brother. The mischievous look that could almost always be found on his face was nowhere to be seen. His eyes were red and swollen from crying.

"Where are we, Mary?" he asked with a sniff.

"We're in the rainforest," she told him.

His eyes widened.

"How did we get here?"

"I don't really know," Mary said. "It was the globe. I guess it does more than just letting us look at the world up close."

Understatement of the year, Mary thought.

Ike stared blankly into the trees as he considered the

unbelievable news. He didn't say anything for a moment, and Mary watched as fresh tears welled up in his eyes.

"I want to go home!" he cried.

Mary typically felt little compassion for her obnoxious brother, but right now, she just wanted to assure him that everything would be alright. She knew exactly how he felt. Despite the hours she'd spent fantasizing about a trip to the Amazon, now that she was here, Mary only wanted to be home. She held onto a branch with one arm, and put her other arm around her little brother, hugging him tightly.

"I know. I want to go home too," she said.

Mary didn't know what else to say, but tried to sound confident and encouraging. She definitely didn't feel that way.

"Come on, let's go find Helen and make sure she's alright, and then we'll find a way to get home," she said, trying to convince herself as much as Ike.

Mary searched for whatever spark of confidence she could find. They were in this mess, and it was all her fault. She was responsible to get them all home. Mary didn't know how, but she was determined to find a way.

CHAPTER SEVEN

Finding Helen

"We have to climb up?" Ike asked, alarmed. "I thought we wanted to get down?"

"What if Helen's above us?" Mary reasoned. "We need to find her first. Then we'll climb down."

Ike wasn't convinced. The thought of climbing higher obviously didn't sit well with him. Not that Mary was looking forward to it either.

"Come on!" she encouraged. "It'll be just like climbing trees at the park."

Mary was beginning to feel less frightened by climbing, but Ike was clearly still petrified.

"Okay, well then why don't you stay here," Mary offered,

starting to climb. "I'll check above us, and you can wait for me."

"Wait! Don't leave me," said Ike with alarm.

Cautiously, he stood on the limb.

"Look above you," Mary said, gesturing toward the sunlight that filtered through the leaves. "We were together when we fell. See how some of the branches are broken in a path that leads directly up? We did that. Helen's either somewhere right above us, or straight below us. If we start at the top and climb down this line of broken branches, we'll find her."

Ike nodded, and Mary hoped she was right. She climbed past Ike, leading toward the treetop. Ike climbed slowly, testing each branch as Mary had done at first.

Mary moved forward, concentrating so intently on her climbing that she didn't notice when something unexpectedly appeared before her face. She almost let go in surprise. It was long and thin, and dangled from a clump of leaves. At first thinking it might be a snake, Mary quickly realized it wasn't alive. It was a green, canvas strap.

What was it doing here? Mary reached out and gave the strap a slight tug. As soon as she did, a backpack materialized and tumbled from the branch above.

"What is it?" Ike asked.

"Grandpa's backpack!" Mary said excitedly. "It's the one

we found in his travel case. I was wearing it when we touched the globe. I must've come off as we fell."

Mary remembered something else.

"Ike! The machete! Were you still holding it?"

Ike thought for a moment.

"I think so," he said, unsure. "But I probably dropped it if I was."

With luck, it fell through the trees and was somewhere on the ground below. The thought gave Mary a little hope, helping to fend off the despair she felt every time she thought about their impossible situation.

The higher she climbed, the thinner the branches grew. Mary was getting close to the top. It made her nervous, but she wouldn't stop until she found Helen or reached the top.

Finally, Mary reached a point where she could peek her head out above the treetop. Like a prairie dog emerging from a hole, her head emerged above the canopy.

The amazing view nearly took her breath away, and made Mary suddenly feel incredibly small. She was surrounded by a vast sea of green leaves that stretched as far as she could see. The sun shone down on the trees, creating a shimmering brightness. Mary knew that most of the sunlight would never fully penetrate the thick canopy and reach the rainforest floor. But up here, everything was bright and alive. She watched in awe as hundreds of magnificent, colorful birds soared in and out of the trees.

"Wow!" she whispered.

It hit her that she was finally here. She was actually in the rainforest. For a brief moment, Mary put her fears aside and drank in the fact that she was living her dream.

It didn't last long. Mary's mind returned to Helen, and she reluctantly tore away from the bewitching view.

"That was amazing!" Mary told Ike, who'd been waiting a few limbs below. "You really should climb up and see for yourself. Green trees stretching on forever!"

"So, you really like leaves, eh?" Ike asked.

Mary laughed, something she rarely did at Ike's sarcasm. Right now, she was just happy for any sign that he was getting back to his usual self.

"No thanks, anyway," he continued. "I'm fine just getting down as soon as we can."

"Alright," Mary said, winking at her brother. "Let's find Helen."

Mary led the down along the path of broken branches, all the while calling out for Helen. There was no reply, though the constant noise of the rainforest made it hard to hear anything other than chattering monkeys, squawking birds, and humming insects.

The further they went, the more Mary began to fear the worst. They'd been climbing for a while, still without any sign of her best friend. Eventually they'd run out of branches.

"I see her!" Ike suddenly cried out.

"Where?" Mary asked, frantically searching.

Ike pointed, and sure enough, Mary spotted Helen's legs draped over a branch below. Her heart leapt with encouragement, and she scrambled toward Helen as quickly as she dared. As the rest of Helen's body came into view, Mary saw that her eyes were closed, and she lay very still. She hoped with all of her heart that Helen was only unconscious.

Mary was almost to Helen when Ike grabbed her by the shirt.

"Wait!" he cried.

"What is it?" she asked, confused.

Ike had a look of sheer panic on his face as he stared in Helen's direction. It didn't take long to see why. A bright green snake was uncoiling from a branch just near Helen's head, and moving directly toward her.

"An emerald boa!" Mary said in amazement.

She'd never seen such a brilliantly-colored snake before. It was beautiful.

"What are we going to do?" Ike said, frightened. "What if it eats her?"

Mary laughed out loud. The snake was big, but probably no more than three or four feet long. Helen was far too large to become prey for a snake like this.

"Don't worry," Mary assured her brother. "It's probably just curious about what landed in its tree. Helen's way too big to eat."

"Really?" Ike asked.

"Definitely," Mary replied. "But let's wait a moment anyway until it goes on its way. Sometimes snakes will strike if they feel threatened."

"Okay," Ike said, sounding not at all comforted by Mary's words.

Mary looked closely at Helen and thought she could see her chest rising and falling. She longed to rush forward and make sure Helen wasn't seriously injured. But for the moment, Mary waited. In fact, she actually hoped that Helen stayed unconscious for just a few moments more. Helen *hated* snakes. Waking up to monkeys pawing at her face was bad enough for Mary. Helen waking to find a large, bright green boa constrictor staring into her eyes would be far worse.

Ike whimpered as the exploring serpent slid particularly close to Helen's face. Every few seconds, the snake's forked, purplish tongue darted in and out. Mary knew the snake was just exploring her surroundings, much like the way that humans taste, touch, and smell. But when that narrow tongue flicked out and touched Helen's face, even Mary shuddered a little. What would Helen do if she knew what was happening? Hopefully, one day Mary could get a kick out of teasing Helen about this.

The boa slithered over Helen's unconscious form a few more times, then finally moved onto another branch. As soon as the boa was far enough away, Mary quickly climbed down. She sighed with relief as she confirmed that Helen was indeed breathing. Scanning her friend, Mary couldn't see any blood or other serious injuries. Miraculously, they'd all survived falling into the tree relatively unscathed.

"Try and wake her up," Ike said.

Mary paused, wondering for a moment how she'd break the news to Helen.

"What do you think she'll say when she wakes up?" Mary asked.

Ike shrugged.

"I dunno. Probably threaten to kill you or something."

Mary laughed nervously. In truth, Ike might not be that far off. Mary was always uncomfortable when Helen's bad temper made an appearance.

"We'll have to wake her up anyway," Ike said. "We might as well get it over with."

Mary nodded, and steeled herself as she reached out and gently shook Helen in an attempt to rouse her. She didn't respond at first, looking as comfortable and relaxed as if she were sound asleep in a big, soft bed, rather than stuck laying on uncomfortable branches. Mary tried harder, and finally, Helen began to stir.

"Mary?" she asked as her eyes fluttered open. "What on earth is going on?"

"Well … " she began, unsure of how to break the news.

But there was no reason to postpone the truth. Taking a deep breath, Mary explained the entire situation. Helen sat up, completely silent as she listened.

Helen didn't act alarmed at all to learn that she was high up in a tree. She sat silently, not saying a single word until Mary had finished.

"Are you okay?" Mary asked, nervous about Helen's silence.

Helen closed her eyes for a moment as if pondering the situation. In an instant, her eyes flew open, burning with rage. All calmness completely disappeared.

"Mary, I'M GOING TO KILL YOU!" she screamed.

Birds and monkeys screeched all around them, echoing Helen's yelling.

"Told you so," Ike said.

"I'm … I'm sorry," was all Mary could say.

She'd seen Helen mad, but never like this.

Unsure of what to do, Mary slowly moved away. Helen didn't look at her, instead staring off into the leaves, her face seething with anger.

"I promise I'll find a way to get us home," Mary said, hoping for a response from her friend.

None came.

Mary tried desperately to think of what else to say. She knew their survival was her responsibility. But beyond that, she was at a loss of what to say. She only knew that now definitely was NOT the right time to tell Helen about the snake.

CHAPTER EIGHT

How to Get Down?

As Mary waited for Helen's anger to fade, she regretted not just giving the old janitor the globe. Maybe everything would've been better that way. Helen and Ike probably thought so.

At the same time, Mary knew that would've been a mistake, especially now that she understood what the globe actually did. Mary didn't even want to imagine what the power of the globe could be used for in the wrong person's hands.

The globe.

"That's it!" she cried out as the realization hit her like a thunderbolt.

"What?" Ike asked.

"The globe!" Mary said. "What happened to it?"

It had been in her hands when they arrived. Mary hadn't been able to see it, but she still felt it until just before they fell into the tree.

"If it transported here to the rainforest with us, then maybe we can use it to get back home!" she declared, excitement filling her as the idea formed.

As soon as she said it, the hopeful thought was replaced by a horrifying one. What if it didn't travel with them? Mary had no idea how it actually worked. For all she knew, they might have transported while the globe went back to the warehouse. The janitor could've just picked it up and walked away.

That thought was worse than anything Mary could've imagined. If true, then all of her efforts to protect the globe would have been for nothing.

At the suggestion of a possible quick way home, Helen's anger started to melt away.

"That's great!" she said. "Then let's get down so we can look for it."

"Sure," Mary said, worried as she continued to think of the globe in the janitor's hands.

"What is it?" Helen asked, noticing Mary's frown.

"What if the globe didn't travel with us? What if it stayed in the warehouse instead? If the janitor has it, who knows how he'll use it?"

"We'll find the globe," Helen said, reassuringly. "I'm sure it's here somewhere."

"And what if it's not?" Ike asked, picking up on Mary's worry.

"Then we'll have to rely on your sister to get us out of here. Who knew that her useless knowledge of the rainforest might just pay off someday?" Helen replied.

Mary smiled. Maybe Helen might actually forgive her after all.

"Then let's find a way out of this tree," Mary said.

"And then what?" Ike asked.

"We'll look for the globe on the ground. If it's not here, then we can't waste any more time. We'll need to gather survival supplies. Then, we'll need to make our way toward the river. Our best bet is to get to the water as soon as possible, and hope we see a passing boat that can help us," Mary proposed.

"Sounds like a plan," Helen agreed. "But how are we supposed to get down? I'm not going to volunteer to do a swan dive and test how soft the ground is."

"What about vines?" Ike suggested. "If we can find some,

we can climb down, just like we're using ropes."

"Ha! I'd like to see that, Tarzan!" Helen teased.

Mary trembled with anxiety at hearing Ike's suggestion. The thought of dangling precariously on a vine with a hundred feet of nothing between her and the ground her wasn't very pleasant. But was there any other way? They weren't going to find a ladder.

They searched for vines along the lower branches, but didn't find anything in their tree.

"I'll try next door," said Helen.

Mary shuddered as Helen casually jumped from their tree to the branches of the neighboring tree. She took a gulp and did her best to follow.

"Hey, look at this!" Helen shouted, after a couple of minutes. "Will these work?"

Mary peered through the leaves and found her friend reaching from a lower limb, with half of her body precariously dangling about fifty feet above the jungle floor. Mary instinctively clamped her eyes shut and turned away, too nervous to even look.

When Helen didn't scream or indicate that she was falling, Mary reluctantly cracked an eye looked in Helen's direction.

"This might just work," said Helen, who reached out and

grabbed one of several long, droopy, rope-like vines.

They didn't look like the vines Mary had envisioned. She imagined green, leafy vines, like those in cartoons. These were part of the actual tree, and were brown like the tree's bark. Helen wiggled a vine back and forth. It swayed, but was stiffer than a rope would've been. The wood-like vines stretched down, nearly to the rainforest floor.

"What do you think?" Helen asked, as she tested out a few vines by tugging on them as she hung from the limb. "They seem strong enough to hold us."

"I think this will work," Mary said, carefully crossing into the neighboring tree and covering her nervousness with fake excitement.

"Well, let's do it then," Helen said, eagerly. "No use waiting. This vine feels the strongest to me. Who's going first?"

"Not it!" called Ike.

Mary knew that she should probably take the lead, but said nothing. In the moment of truth, with the ground plainly visible far below, Mary wondered if she'd actually be able to go through with it.

"Oh fine," Helen said. "I'll go first. You two are real wimps, you know?"

Helen stretched out her shirt sleeves and covered the

palms of her hands. She leaned down and took ahold of the vine.

"See you at the bottom!" she said, shooting a crazy smile at Mary and Ike.

And with that, she dropped. No, Helen *jumped* off the lower limb of the giant tree. It only took a few seconds before she reached the ground. Helen slid down the vine like a fire pole, twirling as she went. When she reached the end, she let go and landed safely on her feet.

"Now THAT was fun!" Helen shouted up at them from down below.

Mary and Ike stared in disbelief at their daredevil friend.

"Are you okay?" Mary yelled down, still unable to believe what she'd just seen.

She knew that Helen was fearless, but who, with any shred of sanity, would just jump out of a tree like that?

"I'm fine," she yelled back. "It's a little rough on the hands, though, so be careful."

Mary turned her brother.

"Ike, I think you should go next."

Ike looked back at her incredulously.

"No way! You go!"

"We both have to go down at some point," Mary reasoned. "What if I go first, and then you decide not to? I don't want you stuck up here."

Mary wondered if she wasn't just looking for any excuse to delay her own climb.

"I'm not a baby!" Ike countered. "I just don't want to go yet, that's all!"

"Are you two chickens going to just sit up there all day?" Helen yelled from far below. "Don't worry! You'll be fine. I promise I'll catch you if you fall."

"Oh, alright!" Ike finally relented. "I'll go. But no way am I going to pull a stunt like Helen."

Ike cautiously slipped his legs off the limb, and slowly started to inch his way down the vine. He hugged the vine with both arms and legs, hanging on for dear life. Moving as slowly as a sloth, Ike scaled down, inch by inch.

It took a long time, but Mary didn't mind. The longer he took, the more it delayed her own turn.

At last, Ike reached the bottom. Hanging from the end of the vine, he stretched as close to the ground as possible before letting go. The drop was only a couple of feet, but he still fell right onto his rear end.

"I'm okay!" he yelled, standing up quickly and brushing himself off.

"Now your turn, Mary," Helen called.

It's now or never, Mary thought.

She grabbed the vine, her heart pounding.

I can do this!

Mary's inner will somehow pushed her to action, and she dropped off the branch.

For a moment she just hung there, swinging slightly, suspended far above the ground. She felt like she'd just jumped out of an airplane without a parachute. Both her arms and legs clenched around the vine, which now felt far too thin to support her.

Mary started her climb, a millimeter at a time. She kept her eyes tightly shut, not wanting to think about the distance between her and the ground.

Far below, Mary heard Helen and Ike shouting encouragement. They'd both made the climb. Shouldn't she be able to do it too? Hand over hand, she kept moving. Every inch took her an inch closer to safety.

The shouting grew louder. She was almost there. Mary sped up, gaining confidence yet eager to be done.

Snap!

Without warning, Mary heard the sound. Immediately, she was weightless.

"Mary!" Helen yelled.

The vine that had been tight in Mary's hands was now limp. She was falling!

There wasn't even time to scream. It was over in an instant. Instead of hitting the ground, Mary felt Helen's arms catching her. They both toppled to the forest floor in a heap. Mary opened her eyes, only to see Helen lying next to her, laughing.

"What's the matter? Afraid of heights?" Helen asked.

"Maybe a little," Mary admitted. "What happened?"

"Your vine broke. But you were almost at the bottom anyway. You would've only been slightly injured if I didn't catch you."

"Thanks for doing that," Mary said.

"No problem, what are friends for?" said Helen, laughing, then suddenly deadpanning in mock seriousness. "But don't forget, I'm still going to kill you when we get out of this mess. I just need you to get me home first, so I can kill you properly."

Mary hugged her friend, and she and Helen laughed deeply as they sat in the dirt.

"You girls are freaks!" Ike said. "Come on, let's get out of here!"

CHAPTER NINE

Find the Water

Her moment of joy was short-lived. Despite Mary's hoping, the globe was nowhere to be found. Ike and Helen helped her search everywhere near the tree. But it was no use. It wasn't anywhere on the ground. Her only consolation was finding Grandpa's machete, stuck into the soft rainforest floor like Excalibur in the stone.

"Now the janitor has the globe!" Mary cried out in dismay.

If the janitor had the globe, what would he do with it? Mary felt empty as she contemplated the terrible consequences that might follow.

"Who cares? He can have the stupid thing," Ike said. "All

I want to know is how we're supposed to get home now?"

Mary couldn't even answer. She was too busy fighting back tears.

"Mary, I guess we'll need you to save us after all," Helen said, patting her on the back.

Mary looked up at her friend through tear-filled eyes.

"I don't think—" she started.

"Yes you can!" Helen interrupted. "If anybody can figure this out, it's you!"

Mary didn't know whether Helen was being sincere, or just trying to inspire her. Maybe it was both. Either way, it helped. She latched onto Helen's encouragement.

"I'll try," she feebly committed.

"Alright good! What should we do first?" Helen asked, pressing the momentum.

Mary wiped her eyes and studied her surroundings. The only thing she was sure of was the need to make their way toward the river. But which way was that? Every direction looked the same.

"We need to go south. I think," Mary began, trying to visualize where they might be. "When we using the globe, we were headed toward a major branch of the Amazon River. We would have landed there, but when Ike bumped me, it shifted our position, pushing us to the north."

"Sorry," Ike said. "How was I supposed to know that we were going to get magically dumped here? Plus, aren't you glad we didn't actually land in the river?"

He did have a point. That would have been a disaster. They wouldn't have survived the strong currents of the Amazon.

"So which way is south then?" Helen asked, eager to move.

"I think it's probably this way," Mary said, pointing in one direction.

Then again, was it?

"Or maybe this way," she said, pointing in a completely different direction.

"What if we start walking the wrong way?" Ike asked. "Won't it only take us only deeper into the jungle?"

"You're right," Mary admitted. "Going the wrong direction won't do us any good."

High above the trees, Mary heard rumbling thunder. The sounds of the rainforest grew steadily louder as thousands of raindrops fell down upon the leafy canopy.

"Oh great," Helen said. "We don't know which way to go, and now we're about to get soaked!"

"I'm already soaked with my own sweat," Ike said. "I don't think the rain will make a difference."

"Thanks, Ike," Helen said, not holding back on the sarcasm. "Nothing like a sweat update from you. Any other important bodily functions you'd like to fill us in on?"

"No, wait guys, this is a good thing!" Mary said.

"What, my sweat?" Ike asked.

"No, the rain!" Mary exclaimed. "We'll need to drink as much water as possible whenever we get the chance! Any other water we find will probably make us sick. But the rain might be clean enough."

Mary fumbled through the backpack. She pulled out the two metal canteens.

"These aren't very big, but at least we can hold some water in them. Let's drink as much as possible, then fill these up so we'll have some water to last until the next rainfall. Quick, try to find a steady stream of water coming from a tree," Mary said, eagerly looking around.

"You mean we have to drink rain?" Ike asked.

"Well, you could always drink your own sweat. You just told us you had plenty," Mary suggested with a laugh.

It took a minute to find what she was looking for. A fairly steady stream of rainwater came from a nearby tree. Mary quickly filled a canteen and started drinking.

"Here goes nothing," Helen said, putting the second canteen to her lips.

Helen looked skeptical at first, but raised her eyebrows in satisfaction as she finished off the flask.

"Hmm, not so bad."

"Your turn, Ike," Mary said, handing him a filled canteen.

"Oh, alright!" he said, grabbing the canteen and taking a drink.

Despite his complaining, he filled and drank from the flask multiple times.

When all had finished drinking, Mary filled the canteens again and put them in the bag. She finished just in time, as the brief rainstorm subsided. The sounds of the rain on the canopy faded, and the cries of birds and insects grew louder once again.

Mary watched as pools of water on the ground dispersed or soaked into the soil. Suddenly, a light went on in her head.

"Guys, look at this!" she said, pointing at the ground.

Helen and Ike tried to figure out what Mary was showing them.

"Mary, are you okay?" Helen asked. "I know you get excited about weird stuff and all, but are you sure there wasn't something in that water that's making you see things?"

"It's normal," Ike said. "She's probably just geeking out about mud."

"Well, not exactly the mud," Mary said. "But look at

what the water's doing!"

Most of the water had already soaked into the ground, creating the mud that Ike pointed out. However, enough water had collected in some areas to create small puddles. Raindrops still dripped from the trees and kept the little puddles filled. As these small pools overflowed, the water trickled away in tiny streams. The streams only lasted for a moment or two, then quickly soaked into the rich rainforest soil.

"I still don't get—" Helen started.

"See if there are other little streams of water like this!" Mary ordered. "And check which direction they're flowing."

Helen and Ike looked at one another and shrugged. Though confused, they obeyed, and began to search per Mary's orders. Together they found a few more pools of collected water. In each case they observed the same phenomenon. They had to look quickly, but it was enough.

"All the streams flow in that same direction," she said, pointing.

"So?" Ike said. "What difference does that make?"

"It's south!" Mary said, triumphantly. "Or at least, it's toward the river, and the direction we want to go."

"How do you know that?" Ike asked, confused.

"The ground here isn't completely flat." Mary explained.

"There's always a low point in a river basin. That's how the river knows where to flow. I remember reading about how all water runs to the lowest part of the land, forming rivers. Even this rainwater is finding its way to the Amazon."

"It sounds smart enough to me, Professor," Helen said. "Should we get going then? I'd like to be home before dinner."

Mary strained to get another look at the sky through the canopy. Even without a clear view, Mary knew that night was coming. Before long, they'd be in the middle of a pitch-black rainforest.

"Are we going or what?" Helen asked, impatiently.

"No," Mary replied. "It's too risky. We'll need to wait until morning."

CHAPTER TEN

Camping

"Say what?" Ike asked, his eyes bulging. "You mean, sleep outside?"

"It'll be just like camping!" Mary replied, hoping to make it sound exciting.

It didn't work. The looks Helen and Ike gave her said that they weren't in the mood for joking around.

"Look," Mary continued, "We'll be outside all night anyway. If we start walking now, we'll either get lost in the middle of a completely dark jungle, or we'll make it to the river and it will be dark there too. There won't be any boats passing at night."

"But won't we be safer near the water?" Ike wondered.

"What if something in the rainforest tries to eat us?"

"Where do you think most of the animals live?" Mary replied. "They all hang out near the water, especially the big animals that hunt at night. I think we'll be much safer here."

Mary knew that sleeping in middle of the rainforest, especially as unprepared as they were, wouldn't be easy. But what other choice did they have?

"Well, if we have to stay out here, should we at least build some kind of shelter?" Helen suggested, sounding resigned to their fate.

"Good idea!" Mary said.

She looked around to see what they might use.

"How about a teepee made out of sticks?" Ike proposed. "There are plenty of those around."

Mary nodded.

"That'll work. Let's gather as many good sticks as we can. Be careful what you pick up, though. Make sure that there aren't any weird looking frogs, or sna … sn … uh … snaggy … things … " Mary trailed off.

"You were going to say 'snakes,' weren't you?" Helen accused.

Mary ignored her and continued on.

"Just assume that anything you don't recognize might be poisonous. Once we have enough sticks, will make a little teepee. We can use the rain coats from Grandpa's backpack to keep dry. One can be for the floor so we're not sleeping in the wet mud. We'll use the other one to cover the top of the teepee, in case it rains again."

"What about the snakes?" Helen demanded.

Ike was holding back laughter, obviously remembering the boa constrictor slithering over Helen in the tree. Mary shot him a look of warning not to say anything.

"Well," Mary said carefully, not wanting to cause any more alarm, "At least one of us can stay awake and keep watch. If anything comes close, we'll scare it away."

"I'll stay up," Helen offered immediately. "There's no way I'll sleep anyway knowing that a snake might slither over me at any moment."

Ike couldn't take it anymore, and nearly fell over laughing.

"What's your problem?" Helen asked.

"Are you sure you want to know?" he replied.

"Actually, not really," Helen said. "Let's just hurry up and get this tent built. I'd like to get through this night as soon as possible."

Mary knew it was going to be a long, exhausting night. Hopefully they'd still have enough strength to get to the river tomorrow. If needed, they could take turns napping in the daylight as they waited for a boat.

"Why don't we build a fire?" Ike suggested. "That would at least make it feel like camping, and might scare all the jaguars and snakes and whatever else lives here away. Mary, you don't happen to have some matches and maybe some marshmallows in Grandpa's magic bag, do you?"

"Nope," Mary said. "But a fire would be a good idea. It's too bad that everything's so damp around here. Even if we had matches, I'm not sure I could get one started."

"We don't need matches. Just leave the fire to me!" Ike said proudly. "I didn't go through two years of Cub Scouts for nothing! Find me two sticks and I'll rub them together."

"Really?" Helen asked, skeptically. "Now that's something I'd like to see."

"Ike, have you ever made a fire like that?" Mary wondered.

"Not exactly," Ike admitted. "But I've seen it done in movies, so it can't be that hard. You girls go and gather your teepee sticks, and I'll get the fire going."

Ike grabbed a nearby stick and immediately started hacking at it with the machete, trying to carve the end to a point.

The girls giggled at Ike's intensity and left to gather branches. Within ten minutes, they had a small teepee constructed, just large enough for the three of them to sit in overnight. It looked even better than Mary had expected.

They finished just in time. It was rapidly getting darker, and soon they wouldn't be able to see anything at all.

"How's that fire coming, Ike?" Helen asked.

"Well, it could be better … " Ike said, hesitantly.

He was furiously rolling a stick in between his palms, with its point held against thick piece of bark. Despite his efforts, there wasn't even any smoke.

"Oh well, maybe I didn't learn anything in Cub Scouts after all," he said, throwing down his stick and giving up.

"Don't worry about it, brother. It was worth a shot," Mary said, giving him an encouraging pat on the shoulder.

The three of them climbed into the small, makeshift tent. The light was almost gone.

"Helen, I know you said you'd stay up. But it's my fault we're here, so I can keep watch. You two should try to get some sleep," Mary said.

"Oh sure, Mary," Helen replied, "I'll just lay down on this comfortable bed and catch some Zs. The fact that a million things are waiting to crawl on me or kill me at any moment won't bother me at all!"

"I think at this point I'd trade these bugs for a jaguar!" Ike said, as he swatted at insects flying around him.

"Just make sure you swat any mosquitoes," Mary said. "They're actually far more deadly to people in the rainforest than any other animals. Malaria, dengue, yellow fever—"

"Thank you, we get the point!" Helen said, slapping at bugs on her arms.

Mary didn't expect that they'd fall asleep easily, if at all. She was on high alert, worried about all that was unseen in the darkness. It was already impossible to see anything more than a few feet away from the teepee.

"Helen, are you still awake?" Mary whispered, after probably fifteen minutes of silence.

"What do you think?" Helen replied.

"Ike, what about you?" asked Mary.

He didn't answer. Mary didn't know how he'd done it, but she could just hear his deep breathing over the cacophony of the night-time rainforest. Ike was fast asleep.

CHAPTER ELEVEN

Waiting for the Morning

BANG!

Mary started awake. The echoes of a gunshot rang through the dark rainforest. Thousands of noisy animals grew even louder in response to the unnatural sound.

"What was that?" Helen asked, her voice tense with anxiety.

It took a moment for Mary to remember where she was.

"I don't know," she said. "I dozed off, but the sound woke me up."

"It sounded like a gunshot," Helen said. "Why would somebody be shooting a gun at night in the middle of the rainforest?"

Mary had no clue. In her sleepy state, she wondered if the janitor had used the globe to follow them. The thought made her shudder at first, until she realized that he'd have no motive for that, now that he already had what he wanted.

"I don't know," Mary said. "But whoever's out there, I hope they stay away. The last thing we want is for a poacher or hunter to mistake us for an animal or something."

The spookiness of the dark rainforest pressed around Mary at every side.

"I don't know if I'll be able to fall asleep again after that," she whispered.

But she was tired. After half an hour passed, Mary felt herself starting to doze off again. That ended abruptly as a blood-curdling jungle cry came from somewhere in the distance. Goosebumps immediately pricked all over her skin.

"And what was that?" Helen asked in a low, frightened whisper.

Mary was terrified by the unearthly sound.

"A howler monkey, I think," Mary fibbed.

A howler monkey seemed like the least threatening of all the possibilities that flashed through her head.

It didn't help at all that Mary was familiar with some of the folklore of strange Amazonian creatures. She thought of the mapinguary, a large, sloth-like Amazonian version of Bigfoot. It was said to have one giant eye and a gaping mouth full of razor-sharp teeth right in the middle of its abdomen. Even if it was only a tall tale, Mary didn't need much imagination in the darkness. She trembled as she tried to think of more pleasant thoughts.

Gradually, Mary let down her guard, and began to drift off again. She was almost asleep when yet another sound jolted her awake. This time, it came from somewhere much closer.

A large "something" hit against the roof of their shelter. Mary listened as it slid over the raincoat before going silent. Rigid with fear, she sat tensely, not daring to make a sound. She hoped Helen was already asleep. Mary suspected another boa constrictor.

For several minutes, she was on guard, expecting a huge snake to come into their tent at any moment. Luckily, it never came.

The night went on, seemingly forever, and Mary drifted in and out of sleep. At long last, the first lights of morning trickled through the leaves above.

Mary emerged first from the little tent. Helen followed, and stretched as if she'd never stretched before. Helen looked ragged and tired, and Mary knew she didn't look any better.

"I'm going to take a quick look around," Helen

announced. "I've got to move after being cramped up like that all night long."

"Don't go too far. We should probably wake up Ike soon and start for the river," Mary said.

"Relax, mom. I'll be right back," Helen replied, walking into the forest.

Ike still snored. After Mary's rough night, she couldn't understand how her little brother had slept so soundly. As she shook him, he drowsily opened his eyes. Glancing around, a look of dejection crossed his face.

"I was hoping this was all just a dream," he whined. "Is it morning already?"

"Yes," Mary answered, "and I don't know how you were able to sleep all night. Helen and I hardly slept at all."

"Did anything happen during the night?" he asked as he climbed out of the tent.

"Well, funny you should ask," Mary said. "A lot of strange sounds, including one that sounded like a gun firing."

"A gun?" Ike asked, his jaw dropping. "You mean there's somebody out here?"

"Apparently," Mary answered. "But if it's a poacher, then I hope we don't cross paths."

Ike seemed spooked by the idea of someone lurking in the dark rainforest, so Mary didn't mention the other scary sounds.

At that very moment they heard somebody, or something, approaching through the brush.

"Ahhh!" Mary and Ike screamed in unison, both jumping.

"Are you two okay?" Helen said with a laugh, coming into view from behind a large bush.

Mary immediately relaxed.

"Oh good, it's just you," she said.

"Of course it's me. Who else would it be?" Helen retorted.

Mary just shrugged.

"So, now that you two are both up, can we *finally* go to the river?" Helen wondered.

"What about breakfast?" Ike asked.

"Oh sure," Helen replied. "Maybe we could just find the nearest McDonald's."

"Very funny," Ike said. "But seriously, are we going to eat anything? I'm starving!"

"I did find these," Helen said, holding out a few yellowish, oval-shaped fruits, each about the size of an egg. "I saw monkeys eating them, so I figure they're not poisonous."

In her hungry state, Mary thought the fruit looked particularly delicious.

"Dig in!" Helen said, smiling.

"What are they?" Ike asked, picking up a piece and

looking at it skeptically.

"Who knows?" Mary said. "Thousands of plants only grow here in the Amazon. I've never seen this one before."

"There's only one way to find out," said Helen, as she sank her teeth into a piece of fruit.

She chewed for a moment. It wasn't clear by her face whether she liked it or not.

"Well, it's not a peach, but I'm hungry enough to not really care," she said, after swallowing.

Mary ate her fruit. The texture was like a tomato, though not as watery. It didn't have much flavor. But like Helen said, she was hungry, and would take what she could get.

"I'm ready for my second course," Ike said, forcing a fake burp.

"Here's a stick," Helen said, tossing him a branch. "Why don't you go monkey hunting?"

"Come on, let's just make our way to the river," Mary said. "Along the way, we'll keep a lookout for anything else to eat."

Mary packed up the raincoats, and was about to set off, when she remembered something she'd thought of during the night.

"Wait! There's one more thing we need to do," she said.

"What now?" Ike complained.

"We need a way to mark our trail," Mary explained. "I want to make sure we don't end up getting lost or going in circles."

"Leave that to me," Ike said, holding up the machete, which he'd adopted as his own.

He walked to the nearest tree.

"Wait, don't!" Mary cried as Ike held his weapon back, ready to strike.

"What's wrong, Mary?" Helen wondered. "For once, your little brother actually has a good idea."

Mary winced.

"I know," she said, "it's just the idea of hurting one of these trees is hard for me."

"Aww, do you need to hug it one last time before we go?" Ike teased.

Mary realized that it was the right thing to do. It was to save their lives, after all.

"Okay Ike, go ahead. Just try not to cause too much damage," she relented.

With a look of pleasure in his eyes, Ike quickly made a few chops in the surface of the trunk, cutting two distinct grooves. It only took a moment, and left a rough shape of the letter "T" on the surface of the tree.

"T, For the Tucker explorers!" Ike said, triumphantly.

Mary grinned at the sound of that.

"But I'm not a Tucker!" Helen protested.

"Well, nobody's perfect," Ike said. "Besides, the 'Tucker-Washington explorers' is too complicated, and a 'T' is easier to carve than a 'W.'"

"Whatever you say little man," Helen said, rolling her eyes. "Now can we finally go?"

With Ike still laughing, the three explorers set off, leaving the shade of the tree which had left an indelible mark on their lives. Surrounding them was nothing but wild, untouched rainforest. Mary took a deep breath, and hoped with all her might that they were headed in the right direction.

CHAPTER TWELVE

To the River

It didn't take long for things to get really hot. In addition to being hungry, thirsty, and exhausted, Mary was now drenched in sweat. The shade of the canopy provided some relief, but it didn't do anything to stop the humidity.

Ike was having fun with the machete, cutting through every plant that blocked their way in the dense jungle. He stopped at every third or fourth tree and eagerly carved another 'T' into the trunk. Mary still grimaced with every chop he took, but she knew it would keep them traveling in the right direction. By lining up two or three of the marked trees still within her line of sight, Mary used them as guideposts to ensure that they were headed in a straight line.

Mary hoped they'd reach the river quickly. Every step

grew harder and heavier. Being tired and hungry didn't help. After a nearly sleepless night in the rainforest, Mary felt like she'd topple over and pass out at any moment. Two or three grueling hours of walking and marking trees passed, still without any sign of the river.

"Are we there yet?" Ike asked for the hundredth time.

Mary was too weak to even answer. When would this end?

Her ears perked up. She heard what sounded like rushing water up ahead. Excited, and with a burst of new energy, Mary jogged forward. Could it be what she thought it was?

A moment later, Mary emerged from the forest and found herself standing on the bank of the massive Amazon River. She gaped at the magnitude of the enormous waterway. The muddy brown current pushed along as a steady, moving wall of water. Entire uprooted trees drifted by, probably coming all the way from somewhere high in the Andes Mountains. No power on earth would be strong enough to stop this river.

Ike and Helen emerged from the forest and joined Mary, breathing heavily.

"Finally!" Helen gasped.

"Now that's one gigantic river!" Ike said, in awe. "I've never seen anything like it."

Mary wanted to collapse, but seeing the river momentarily took her attention away from how she felt. Finally viewing the Amazon—really seeing it in all of its glory—was enough to take her breath away.

Mary knew that the river would only get bigger the closer it got to the Pacific Ocean, more than one thousand miles away. In fact, they were closer to the beginning of the Amazon than to its end. If the river was already this big, how much bigger would it get?

After a few moments of watching the river, Helen turned to Mary.

"Now what?" she asked.

"We have two options. We can wait here, taking turns resting and keeping watch for boats. Or, we can follow the current downstream. We'll eventually find a city or village," Mary said, not adding her silent thought of "*I hope.*"

"I vote for the resting option," Ike said quickly.

"What's your problem? You're the one who actually got to sleep," Helen said. "You should be fine."

"Not everybody can be a superhero like you," Ike retorted.

"We could also do a combination of both options," Mary suggested. "We could rest here for a few hours, and then start walking if we don't see anything by then."

Everybody agreed without complaint. Despite having gone the whole evening without real sleep, Helen volunteered to take the first watch. Mary feebly tried to argue, but was secretly grateful for Helen's offer.

Mary found a nice patch of soft, long grass. Bugs buzzed around her, but she was too tired to care. She'd only been laying down for a few minutes when sleep overtook her.

Mary's dreams were a combination of monkeys climbing all over her, falling out of trees, and watching as a strong river current carried everything away like a flash flood. She watched helplessly as trees, animals, and people were washed down the raging river.

Her dream changed, and so did the river. Now, instead of carrying people swiftly away, it was filled with boats. Mary jumped up and down on the shore, waving her arms and screaming at the top of her lungs. She desperately wanted to get their attention, but to her dismay, not a single boat stopped or even acknowledged her.

She saw a figure on one of the otherwise empty boats. Blurry at first, as the boat drifted closer, a person came into view. The old janitor, stared back at her, an evil look in his eye.

"Looking for this?" he asked, holding the globe high into the air, then throwing back his head in malicious laughter.

Mary began screaming uncontrollably.

"That's not yours!" she cried. "Bring it back!"

The janitor continued to laugh, and his boat disappeared among the throngs of empty vessels crowding the river. Mary still screamed as he disappeared, but it made no difference. She felt completely helpless, watching him sail away.

Something shook Mary's body, and suddenly the screaming voice was not her own.

"Mary! Mary! Wake up!"

Mary's eyes snapped open. Helen stood over her, calling her name.

"What is it?" Mary asked, as she regained consciousness. "Did you see the boat? Where did he go?"

"What boat? Where did who go?" Helen asked, puzzled.

Mary stared at the sky for a moment, realizing it was all a dream.

"The janitor," she said. "I had a dream about him taking the globe down the river, and I couldn't stop him."

"You were screaming in your sleep. You sounded like you were dying or something!" Helen still had alarm visible in her eyes.

Mary tried to collect her thoughts.

"It was just a nightmare," she admitted.

Helen sat quietly next to her.

"It'll be okay," she promised. "We'll find a way to get the globe back, once we're home."

Mary nodded and smiled appreciatively at her best friend.

"How long was I out?" she asked.

"Probably about three hours," Helen said, yawning, and obviously on the brink of exhaustion herself.

"Really?" Mary said, completely surprised. "It only felt like a couple of minutes!"

She sat up, and saw Ike curled up nearby. How did he sleep so much?

"Let's trade places," Mary suggested, despite the groggy protestations of her body. "You really need some rest too."

"No, I'm fine," Helen said, again through a huge yawn.

"Come on," Mary said. "I know you're Wonder Woman and all, but you still need sleep."

Helen just shrugged.

"Lay down," Mary said in a motherly tone, pointing at the spot where she had just been sleeping.

Helen just mumbled to herself as she laid down and closed her eyes.

Mary considered waking Ike and forcing him to keep watch with her. Deciding it wasn't worth it, she instead took a seat on a rock near the water's edge. A pleasant breeze began to blow, cooling Mary a little in the humidity.

Looking for something to do, Mary opened up Grandpa's knapsack. The raincoats and the flasks had already been helpful. What else could they use?

Rummaging, she saw that it contained a piece of narrow

rope, coiled up and tied on the end, an old metal can opener, unfortunately without any cans to open, and a tiny garden shovel. One item in particular drew Mary's interest. It was the small, leather-bound book. Carefully, Mary examined the book, turning it over in her hands. It didn't have a title, and was tied shut with a leather strap. Unlike the other items, it wasn't worn and used. In fact, it appeared to be almost brand new.

Curious to know more, Mary carefully untied the strap, and opened to the book's first page. In a flowing cursive handwriting, Mary read:

My Dearest Ephraim,

I know how much you love your work. I can see the joy in your eyes whenever you return from one of your adventures. I wish I could share them with you. But even though my body won't let me travel, I long to be a part of it all. Perhaps in this book you can record your adventures in a way that we'll all be able to enjoy, for years to come. I know one day Lewis will appreciate being able to read all about his father—the daring explorer and fearless globetrotter!

With love,
Your Lilly

Mary couldn't believe it! She was reading words written by her grandmother. Grandma Lilly died before Mary was born, according to Mom, after a household accident. Other than that, Mary knew next to nothing about her. Neither Dad nor Grandpa could speak of her without tears, and she was seldom mentioned as a result. Mary always wondered what she was like. Did this journal contain any clues? Mary eagerly flipped to the next page.

Sure enough, there was an entry, this time in her grandfather's unmistakable, narrow handwriting. It wasn't as beautiful as Grandma Lilly's, but it was legible. The page contained a single, short entry.

July 29th, 1989

Well, Lilly, if you want me to write about my adventures, then that's just what I'll do. I'm back in the Soviet Union, in Russia this time. As usual, my lucky globe whisked me here just as safely and smoothly as ever. I'm glad it's summer, because here in Yakutia, in the northeastern part of the country, beyond Siberia, the winters get so cold that you can't stay outside for more than a few minutes. Your eyelashes freeze together and your tongue starts to sting. But summertime is beautiful. Who would have ever thought that such a desolate

*winter land could bloom so beautifully in the spring? And
the people are just as friendly as ever. I'm looking for clues
and evidence on the origin of the Yakut people, and for any
other treasures I might pick up along the way. Not much to
report yet, but I'll be back and write more. Don't you worry,
my dear Lilly. Your wish is my command!*

Mary flipped to the next page, fascinated by the story
and keen to read more. But it was blank. Mary thumbed
through the rest of the pages. They were blank too. If fact,
there wasn't another mark throughout the rest of the book.

Mary frowned. Why hadn't Grandpa written more? The
empty pages shed no more light about either his adventures
or about Grandma. No wonder the journal looked so new.

It took Mary a moment to figure out why nothing else
had been written. Looking back to Grandpa's short entry
from Russia, she noted the date. Mary might not know much
about Grandma Lilly, but she recognized that day. July 29th,
1989. The same day of Grandma's accident and death.

Grandpa was traveling when she died. Did this have
something to do with Dad's cold relationship with Grandpa,
and his dislike for travel? Mom had once mentioned something
about Dad being only a teenager when Grandma died, and
how he had to deal with arrangements for Grandma's funeral

and burial by himself. It seemed to Mary that something like that could change a person.

Mary didn't know what had actually happened, but she felt she was beginning to understand. A tear trickled down her cheek. She wished that Grandma were still alive. Maybe then they could have all been traveling the world together, as a happy family.

Mary laid on her back and stared at the sky. Here she was, lost in the middle of the Amazon, missing a grandmother she never knew, and dreaming about what might have been. Life wasn't fair sometimes.

She wiped her eyes, and felt resolve come over her. Somehow, she'd change things back. She'd fix Dad and Grandpa's relationship. She'd honor Grandma's memory, not by hiding from the world, but by embracing it. She'd do so many things when she got home.

If she got home.

Mary's emotions wore her out just as much as her morning march through the rainforest. Without even noticing, she closed her eyes, and fell asleep again.

CHAPTER THIRTEEN

Nightfall

Raindrops on her face startled Mary awake. With a gasp, she sat up, realizing that she'd fallen asleep. Helen and Ike were also stirring. Her stomach growled with hunger, her throat was dry, and her head was pounding.

How long had she slept? Mary desperately hoped that she hadn't missed any passing boats. She felt so guilty for allowing herself to drift off.

As she stood, Mary tried to guess the time. The sun was already lowering into the western horizon. They'd likely only have a few more hours of light. Mary shuddered at that thought of another night spent camping in the jungle.

"Did you see any boats?" Helen asked, walking up to

Mary's side. "I'm going to go ahead and guess no, given that we're still here."

"Actually," Mary admitted sheepishly, "I kind of fell asleep again."

"You what?" Ike said, sounding outraged as he joined the girls.

"Excuse me?" Helen shot back. "You've got no place to complain. You've been asleep since we got here!"

It was nice of Helen to defend her, but Mary knew they both felt as disappointed as she did. She'd hoped they would've at least gotten somewhere by now.

"Alright then," Helen said. "Since we're all rested up, should we start making our way along the river?"

"If we go downstream, it'll probably give us the best chance of finding somebody that will be able to help," Mary suggested, eager to do anything that felt like progress.

Once again they set off, following the Amazon downriver. The riverbank was mostly clear of trees, making it much easier to walk than it had been in the jungle. Mary supposed this meant that the river at times rose high enough to cover the area where they now stood.

Ike continued to mark their path by carving Ts into the trees closest to the river. Mary didn't think it was necessary, but Ike insisted that he needed to keep up his "machete skills."

They came upon a grove of palm-like trees, several of which were no longer standing. Dozens of tree trunks were laying side by side, and Mary wondered what had caused so many to fall in one place. Ike approached one of the downed trees. Pretending he was a knight, he lifted the machete high above his head.

"I slay thee, foul tree!" he cried, as he brought the blade down against the fallen trunk.

As he did, it cracked open, much to Mary's surprise. Her surprise turned to understanding as she looked at the splintered tree trunk, which revealed a rotting center.

"Hmm, I guess I don't even know my own strength," Ike said, with satisfaction.

"That's for sure," Helen said, laughing. "Nice superpowers you've got there."

"You're just jealous of my machete skills," Ike shot back. "You'll thank me when I end up using this to save your life."

"Whatever, little man," Helen said.

They were about to continue onward, when Mary noticed something white moving within the rotted tree trunk. She moved in for a closer look and picked up a piece of the broken wood. When she saw what was underneath, she leaped back in surprise.

It was a fat, white, wriggling grub. It looked like a

caterpillar, and was as big as Mary's thumb. After getting over her initial shock, Mary discovered not only one, but several of the creatures writhing throughout the rotten wood. Their bodies were smooth and white, and each had a beady, jet-black head.

Helen came up to see what Mary was looking at.

"What is it this time ... yeeow! What on earth is that?" Helen screeched as she jumped back, repulsed by the grubs.

Mary felt her stomach rumble with hunger.

"Dinner?" she suggested.

Mary couldn't believe she was even considering it, and felt sick the moment the word left her lips. But her stomach knew she needed to eat, and she was beginning to believe that they wouldn't find anything else.

"No way, not a chance!" Helen ferociously protested. "What is this, *The Lion King*? I'd rather starve than eat one of those ugly things!"

"I don't want to eat them either," Mary argued, "But what else are we going to eat? I saw a documentary where people from the Amazon eat these things all the time. It might be gross, but it won't kill us. Starving will."

"Can't Helen just go find some more fruit?" Ike suggested.

"I'll do it if I can avoid having to eat bugs," Helen said, angrily kicking at the tree trunk.

"What if you don't find any right away? We haven't seen any for a while," countered Mary.

She still couldn't believe she was trying to convince them to eat the grubs.

"Fine, but I still don't want to eat that." Helen said.

"Neither do I," said Ike, walking toward the river. "I'll go stab a fish with my machete instead."

"Don't you dare!" said Helen. "If you drop that thing, I'll make you swim after it."

"Fine, then I'll just use my hands," Ike relented.

Mary knew she wasn't going to convince them with words. There was only one thing she could do. Plucking up enough courage, she reached down and grabbed one of the grubs. It squirmed between her fingers, and Mary tried not to think about what she was doing. She knew that she had to it quickly, or else she'd never be able to go through with it. Wincing, Mary squeezed off the bug's black head, leaving the white, headless body still wriggling back and forth.

"Disgusting!" yelled Ike.

"Mary, don't do it!" Helen cried.

She couldn't stop now. Mary hastily shoved it in her mouth. She gagged reflexively, but forced herself to ignore the little wiggling legs against the insides of her cheeks. Straining, she swallowed the grub whole.

"Well?" Ike finally asked, revulsion on his face. "How was it?"

Mary took a gulp.

"Not at all like chicken," she said, then smiled. "But, it wasn't completely terrible. Who's next?"

Mary decided not to mention how she could still feel the grub squirming from inside her stomach. It kind of tickled, actually.

"Oh no," Helen said. "Not a chance! This is your thing alone. Just because you've turned into some crazy jungle person, there's no way you're going to stick one of those slimy things in my mouth."

"Suit yourself," Mary said. "If you're too *afraid*, that just leaves more for me."

She picked up another grub, popped off the head, and then swallowed it down. It was much easier the second time around.

"I said, you're not going to talk me into this!" Helen yelled.

But Mary knew it was all over. She'd accused her competitive friend of being afraid, and Helen could never back down from even an implied dare.

"Remember when I told you I was going to kill you?" Helen said. "Well, this just makes it all the more certain."

With that, Helen, her eyes clenched tight, reached down

and grabbed a grub. Just as Mary had done, she pulled off the head and popped the wriggling body into her mouth. Jumping up and down, Helen screamed within her closed mouth as she swallowed.

"See, that wasn't so bad, was it?" Mary asked.

Helen just glared at her, anger and disgust alternating in her eyes.

"You girls are nuts!" Ike said, shaking his head in disbelief.

Mary started gathering up the grubs. She wanted to take full advantage of the food source while they had it. She ate four more, and even Helen forced herself through the ritual a few more times. She made less and less of a fuss with each grub she ate.

Mary didn't try to convince Ike. She knew her little brother couldn't be goaded like Helen. He did, however, hate feeling left out. Sure enough, after seeing the girls eat multiple grubs, he finally joined in.

"Here goes nothing," he said, as he tossed a headless grub into his mouth.

He considered as he swallowed.

"Hmm, that's actually kind of good!"

Ike reached for another and another, eventually eating more grubs than Mary and Helen combined.

After they'd eaten their fill, Mary looked at the shattered

tree trunk and found herself suddenly laughing uncontrollably. The rainforest sure was doing strange things to them.

Mary led the way as they walked for another hour. Ike searched more fallen logs along the way, hoping to discover more grubs.

Eventually, Mary realized they were unlikely to find a boat before nightfall. Not a single one had passed. As terrible as the thought was, she knew they'd need to spend another night in the forest.

"Does this mean we'll have to camp again?" Ike complained.

"Unless you want to try and walk in the dark," Mary reasoned. "I'd hate to accidentally fall into the river. The caimans, anacondas, and piranhas probably won't mind, though."

"That wouldn't bother me," said Ike, sounding pouty. "I'll make friends with them."

"You do realize we're talking about crocodiles, gigantic snakes, and fish with razor sharp teeth that could turn you into a skeleton if they wanted, don't you?" Helen asked.

"Ignore him, he's just trying to be obnoxious," Mary replied.

Ike laughed and pretended to call out to the piranhas in the water.

"Here, fishy, fishy, fishy!"

"Could we at least camp on the riverbank this time?" Helen asked.

"We could," Mary said. "But I think it would be safer to go back into the jungle. There will be fewer animals and mosquitoes."

After some discussion, they decided to walk into the jungle for about ten minutes, searching for a good place to camp. This way, they wouldn't be right on the river, but they'd still be close enough to find their way back in the morning.

"Here we go again!" Mary said, trying to sound cheerful as she led the way.

She started into the jungle. After a few steps, she could tell that something wasn't right. A strange feeling filled the air. It felt like someone, or something, was watching her. Mary glanced back at Helen and Ike. They both stood still, frozen in their tracks.

"What's wrong?" Mary asked.

Both Ike and Helen were looking beyond Mary, with wide eyes, into the forest. Their terrified faces looked like they'd just seen a ghost.

"I saw something moving through the trees," Helen said in a low voice.

"I saw it too," whispered Ike.

Goosebumps prickled all over Mary's body. She couldn't

help but feel that something bad was about to happen.

Slowly, Mary turned, trembling in fear as she wondered what she might see. But as she scanned the jungle, she saw nothing but trees.

Yet the strange feeling was still there. And the rainforest sounded different too. The usual noise of birds and insects had almost completely died away, leaving an eerie silence.

"Anything?" she asked Helen and Ike.

"I don't see it," Helen admitted.

"Neither do I," said Ike.

Mary tried to loosen up. It was probably nothing. The rainforest could be a mysterious place, but it didn't mean that they were in danger.

Mary cautiously took another step into the forest.

"Look out!" Helen suddenly cried.

Mary felt Helen push her, sending her sprawling to the jungle floor. Helen and Ike crashed to the ground with her.

As she fell, Mary caught a glimpse of a large, yellow and black animal leaping from the forest. It was a big, muscular cat-like creature, and it let out a deep growl as its paws hit the ground. It had jumped right through the air at the very spot where Mary had been standing just a second earlier, narrowly missing her.

"Jaguar!" Ike yelled.

CHAPTER FOURTEEN

Teeth and Claws

Mary had never been more terrified in her life. The initial attack had happened so fast, and she'd instinctively jumped to her feet after falling to the ground, somehow knowing that it was necessary to survive. Yet now she was trapped, shaking uncontrollably, and hardly able to stand. What was she supposed to do?

The jaguar circled as they stood, cornered, with no way to escape. What was it doing? Mary couldn't figure out why the big cat didn't immediately attack again. The jaguar kept its eyes fixed on them, snarling in a menacing way. Mary couldn't help but feel that it was waiting for just the right moment to pounce.

Amidst the crippling fear, Mary noticed something odd about the jaguar. It limped whenever it stepped on its right-front paw. And was that paw covered in blood?

She didn't have time to dwell on the thought. Her body continued to tremble, and it was hard to even think. Ike still held the machete, but the jaguar would be too fast for it to do any good.

"Let's run for it!" Helen suggested with urgency.

"No!" Mary shot back, her voice hoarse with fear. "Running will just convince it that we're its prey. I think we're stronger together. We should try to scare it away."

Mary screamed at the jaguar as loudly as she could. Helen and Ike joined in. They waved their arms high above their heads. At first, it worked. The startled animal jumped back, moving away from the screaming children. But it wasn't enough to fully convince the jaguar. The cat let out a deep, rumbling roar, and then reversed course, again moving closer to them. Mary had a sickening feeling as she felt the predator slowly inching closer to its prey.

A surge of new fear cropped up in Mary. Her trembling was almost uncontrollable. All she could think to do was scream even louder. Helen and Ike picked up on the urgency. In a flood of bravery, Ike even stepped forward and swung the machete furiously at the big cat. Reflexively, the jaguar took a swipe with its strong paw and knocked the machete from his hands and out of reach.

"Mary, it's not working!" Helen cried.

The jaguar looked more determined than ever as it crouched down, preparing to spring. The world felt like it was in slow motion. Mary braced herself, but it was too much for her to handle. All the screaming and growling blended into dull, unintelligible sounds. Her legs finally gave way and she crumpled to the ground in fear. Curled up in the dirt, she waited with terror to feel sharp claws or teeth ripping into her. She wailed in her mind, though her voice could no longer produce any sound. The fear was completely paralyzing.

Yet the teeth and claws never came. There was no pain. Was it that quick? Was she already dead? Mary didn't know, but she wasn't ready to find out either. She hugged her knees close to her chest, and clenched her eyes shut.

The jaguar roared, but sounded distant. Mary heard a crashing through the brush. There were other sounds too. Human voices? The roars grew fainter, while the voices grew louder.

"Helen?" Mary croaked out, wondering if it were her friend speaking.

But the voices were unfamiliar. They spoke a language

Mary didn't recognize. Someone put a strong hand on her shoulder. Very cautiously, she cracked opened her eyes, not knowing what she'd find.

Before Mary was the face of a man. Firelight from a torch flickered on his cheeks. He spoke in the unknown language. Mary just stared, with no idea of what to say.

He tried once more, this time struggling to speak in Spanish.

"¿*Todo* … *bien*?" he asked.

"*Bien*, we're fine," Helen interjected, helping Mary stand and brushing the dirt and leaves from her. "We're not dead, I mean, *no muerte* … eh … *es más importante*."

They all knew a little Spanish from school, but Helen had always been most successful in the subject.

As Mary shakily stood up, she found not one but two young men holding torches. At hearing Helen's reply in Spanish, they laughed heartily. They turned to one another and began to chatter away, again in the unknown language.

"Taremuku," said one of the young men, turning to the children and pointing to his chest.

"Wueku," said the other, repeating the gesture.

"*Soy* Helen, *y es* Mary *y* Ike," Helen said, introducing them all.

Helen offered her hand to the two young men to shake

it. They each took it with amused looks, and then began to laugh among themselves again. Apparently, they found it comical that this eleven-year-old foreigner carried herself in such a manner.

"*¿Dónde sus padres?*" Taremuku asked.

"Our parents? *No aquí,*" Helen answered. "*Solo nosotros,* we're alone."

The two men exchanged puzzled glances, followed by more unintelligible conversation. They searched the area, holding their torches close to the ground, as if looking for something.

Suddenly, Wueku called out to Taremuku. He pointed at a spot on the ground. Mary followed, curious to see what he'd found. On the surface of a flat stone, she saw a bloody paw print.

"*Yaguar,*" Taremuku said.

He said a few more words in his native language, obviously unsure how to explain in Spanish. When he could see that Mary had no idea what he was saying, he resorted to miming. He held out his hands, as if he were holding a rifle, and imitated the sound of a gunshot. Then, he pointed back at the paw print.

"*Yaguar,*" he repeated.

"The jaguar?" Mary asked, trying to piece together what Taremuku meant.

Since neither he nor Wueku carried guns, she didn't think that they wanted to kill it.

"The gunshot last night," Ike said. "Maybe it was somebody trying to shoot the jaguar?"

"Maybe," Mary said, considering. "I wonder if that's why it tried to attack us. If it's injured, it's probably not able to hunt its usual prey, and could be starving."

"Oh sure," Helen said. "Typical Mary, taking the jaguar's side. You know, that thing did just try to eat you."

"I'm just saying," Mary said.

"But who would have tried to kill the jaguar?" Ike asked.

"A poacher, maybe? Your guess is as good as mine," Mary replied.

Wueku was upset as he looked at the paw print and then pointed toward the forest. He spoke rapidly with Taremuku, and seemed to be on the verge of running into the jungle in the direction that the jaguar had gone. Taremuku grabbed his arm before he could leave, and gestured toward the children.

After a few minutes of rapid and heated conversation between the two, Wueku calmed down. He nodded, and both turned toward Mary, Helen, and Ike.

"*Vamos*," Taremuku said, starting to walk away and waving them to follow.

Mary wasn't sure what to think. They'd just survived a

jaguar attack, thanks to the fortunate appearance of these two young men. Part of Mary was still recovering from the crippling fear of her near-death experience. But they seemed to be offering help. Mary realized that Taremuku and Wueku potentially offered a chance to find their way home. She made up her mind and began to follow them.

The two men walked quickly and silently, leading the children through the rapidly darkening jungle by torchlight. Mary had to jog to keep up.

While trying to avoid tripping over branches or stepping in holes, Mary attempted to get a better view of her saviors. She'd been so shocked in the immediate aftermath of the jaguar attack, that she hadn't noticed some of the peculiarities of Taremuku and Wueku. Clearly they were from some native Amazonian tribe. Though hard to see in the dark, their appearance was nonetheless very striking. For one, they were almost completely naked. Neither wore a shirt, and Wueku only wore a loincloth and was barefoot. Taremuku, on the other hand, was wearing cargo shorts and tennis shoes. Mary noticed a shiny watch strapped to his wrist.

Both had long, dark hair at the back of their heads. The front of their hair was cut short, with bangs making a straight line along their foreheads. Both of their bodies were painted with spots of color here and there, though nothing was too intricate or elaborate.

"What are we doing?" Ike whispered frantically to Mary, as he struggled to keep up. "What if they're cannibals?"

"Cannibals?" Mary said with a laugh, as she swatted her brother across the head. "Do you really think that cannibals wear tennis shoes and wristwatches?

"Maybe," Ike said. "He could have taken them from yesterday's lunch!"

"Ike, I think you've been watching too many zombie movies. We're in the twenty-first century, you know," Mary said.

Helen chimed in.

"I don't care who they are. I'm going to follow them. They're the first people we've seen, and our best chance of getting home. Plus, don't forget that they saved us from becoming jaguar food."

They continued to follow their guides through the trees. This half-jog felt like running a marathon.

Their brisk walk suddenly halted as they reached a branch of the river. Taremuku and Wueku hadn't even broken a sweat, while the three children panted to catch their breath.

Only a few meters from where they stood, Mary saw a long, floating piece of wood in the water. It had a hollow middle, and almost looked like a canoe in the dim light.

"*Vamos*," said Taremuku again, this time indicating that he wanted them to sit in the canoe-like log. As Mary got closer, she saw that it wasn't a log that looked like a canoe after all. It actually was a canoe!

"No thanks," Ike said. "That thing definitely doesn't look safe."

"Maybe he's right," Helen said, nervously. "I don't want to tip over in the river because of that skinny thing."

Mary wasn't sure of what to say. The canoe did look like it could easily capsize. But on the other hand, this was the only opportunity they'd had so far of possibly getting home. Mary decided that once again, she'd need to be brave and do something that she didn't want to do. Without saying a thing, she stepped forward and climbed onto the canoe.

Wueku was already at the front of the boat, and offered a stabilizing hand to Mary. The canoe did feel a bit shaky, but with Wueku's help, Mary was able to balance and sit down safely. Once seated, the boat felt surprisingly secure.

"It's not so bad," she said to Helen and Ike, who still eyed the canoe nervously from the shore.

They both groaned as they relented and joined Mary on the wobbly boat.

"We'll be fine," Mary said, once the other two were seated alongside her. "Taremuku and Wueku are from the Amazon.

They'll know how to use this thing safely."

Mary hoped she was right.

Taremuku was the last to board, and as soon as he'd shoved the canoe away from the bank, he and Wueku began to powerfully stroke at the water with long oars. Within seconds, they found themselves swiftly paddling down the river.

Sitting on the water felt amazingly peaceful. It brought needed relief to their tired bodies and feet. Mary, still tense from the jaguar incident, felt she could finally let her guard down.

She took in the serenity of the moment. They sky had darkened, and the moon was shining brightly, reflecting in shimmering ripples along the surface of the water. The silhouettes of the tall trees flanked either side of the river. Sounds of both the water and of animals in the forest echoed all around. They fit perfectly together, singing to Mary as a sacred hymn.

This was Mary's dream as she had imagined it.

She glanced over at Ike and Helen. Both were slowly nodding off. Mary realized that she also wanted to close her eyes. With the boat still gliding along the river, and the sounds of the jungle surrounding her, Mary drifted like the current, and was soon fast asleep.

CHAPTER FIFTEEN

In the Ticuna Village

M ary awoke naturally, completely refreshed. The shining sun peeked through holes in the canopy and touched her face. She rested alone on a hammock, between two tall trees. How long had she been sleeping? Given how thirsty she felt, Mary wondered if it hadn't been days.

She thought about getting up, but she felt so comfortable. She wanted to stay where she was, enjoying the comfort as long as she could. But soon her dry throat and rumbling stomach became too hard to ignore.

Near the hammock was a large, wooden structure with no walls. Beneath its leaf-thatched roof, Mary spotted Ike and Helen sitting on stumps and hunched over an enormous wooden bowl. As Mary approached, she saw that it was filled with a delicious-looking assortment of fresh fruits and nuts. Ike and Helen were eagerly eating, and didn't notice Mary standing over them, hungrily eyeing the fruit bowl.

"That looks really good," she said, her mouth watering.

"Well, look who decided to join the land of the living!" Helen said as she threw Mary a citrus fruit.

"How long have you been awake?" Mary asked.

"Not very long," Ike said. "I woke up a few minutes ago. A lady came and brought me over here. She didn't say anything, just sat me down and brought out this bowl full of fruit. Helen smelled it, and before I knew it, she was here too, eating my food."

"I'm pretty sure it's meant for us to share," Helen said, tossing a nut in her mouth.

"Have you seen anybody else?" Mary asked.

"Just a few people," Ike said. "They all get a kick out of looking at us. I guess they don't get a lot of random foreign guests."

"A whole group of kids was watching me when I woke up," Helen said. "One came over and started touching my braids, thinking I was asleep. As soon as I sat up, the kids all ran away, screaming and laughing."

"Where do you think we are?" Ike asked, his mouth full of fruit.

"I don't know," Mary admitted. "I mean, it's an indigenous Amazonian village, but I don't know much at all about the tribes who live here."

Studying her surroundings, Mary couldn't help but wonder what it would be like to live in a village like this, spending her entire life in the rainforest. It probably felt ordinary to those who lived here. But not to Mary. Living year after year, always surrounded by the tall, beautiful trees, seemed like paradise.

Peering through the leaves, Mary saw neat little wooden houses, their roofs also thatched with leaves. The homes didn't rest on the ground, but were propped up on short stilts.

Mary also finally got a glimpse of several of the village's occupants. All were busily engaged in something. The women and men were working, carrying pitchers or bundles. The children ran about playing in groups. Everyone looked so happy.

Before long all of the fruit, nuts, and the water from a nearby plastic jug were gone. Mary sat back and enjoyed the moment, satisfied with food, drink, and sleep for the first time since arriving in the rainforest.

"Look!" said Ike, who'd been using the machete to draw pictures in the dirt floor.

A group of children were timidly hiding behind some

nearby brush, clearly hoping for a peek at their strange guests. They giggled and spoke to one another in hushed tones.

"Hello! Don't be shy, come on over!" Mary invited, waving to the children.

They immediately burst into laughter and scattered as quickly as they'd come. Their playful voices rang throughout the village as they romped from one end of the settlement to the other.

A group of adults passed, smiling and greeting the children in their native language. They didn't stop, and Mary began to wonder if there was something they should be doing.

At long last, a group of villagers approached. Mary recognized Taremuku and Wueku. They were joined by an old man, and old woman, and a boy. Unlike the rest, the boy was fully dressed in western clothing, and didn't have the same unique hairstyle of the others. He was a teenager, perhaps three or four years older than Mary. If Mary had seen him walking down the streets of Charleston, she wouldn't have ever guessed that he from the Amazon.

The old man spoke. His twinkling brown eyes were set deep within his sharply wrinkled face. He immediately portrayed a feeling of wisdom and kindness. Standing before Helen, he put his hands on her arms and looked her squarely in the eyes. After a few words, he smiled and bowed his head.

He repeated the ritual with both Ike and Mary. All three of them instinctively bowed and thanked the old man as he finished.

The boy cleared his throat and spoke.

"Honored guests! Our tribal Elder, Meetuku, wishes you welcome to our village. We are of the Ticuna people, and many of our brothers and sisters live in villages throughout the rainforest. Here, we do not often have visitors, but we always welcome those in need."

Mary stared in disbelief.

"You speak English!" Ike proclaimed.

"Yes, I study English in a school in Leticia," said the boy. "My name is Pipieku, but many call me Pepe."

A surge of hope filled Mary, realizing they'd be able to communicate and ask for help.

"I'm Mary, and this is my brother Ike, and our friend Helen. Elder Meetuku, we are very grateful to you and to Taremuku and Wueku for helping us, and for saving our lives."

Mary tried to speak in a mature manner, wanting to show proper respect. She looked at the Elder, rather than Pepe, as she spoke. Mary didn't want to make any mistakes in this culture that she knew nothing about.

Pepe translated her words. The Ticuna Elder listened

patiently, nodding as he did, and replying after a moment of contemplation.

"Meetuku says you are most welcome to stay in our village for as long as you need. You are welcome to our food and to our beds. But, our Elder is very curious to know, how did you come to be here? The Amazon is our home, but it can be very dangerous for those who do not know it well. Where did you come from?"

Mary exchanged glances with Ike and Helen, unsure of how to answer.

"We fell," Helen finally said. "We were traveling by air, but an accident left us stranded in the trees."

"Are others lost in the forest?" Meetuku asked, clearly concerned.

"We're alone," Mary assured him. "And our families are far away. They don't know how to find us. They don't even know that we're here."

Pepe and Meetuku conversed for a long moment. Mary felt she needed to be honest with these people—the Ticuna. After all, they'd saved her life. At the same time, how could she explain the truth? Mary worried she might offend the Ticuna with their impossible story.

"You are too young to fly an airplane alone, are you not?" Meetuku asked.

After another long moment, Mary answered.

"You're right, we didn't come by plane."

Meetuku looked at her deeply, clearly seeking the truth. Once again, Mary glanced at Helen and Ike. Helen nodded for her to go on.

"It's difficult to explain," Mary began. "Honestly, we're not sure how it all happened. We found an object that allowed us to use some sort of, well, magic, I guess. I know it sounds impossible, but it's true. We thought it would only show us the Amazon, and we didn't expect to actually come here."

Pepe looked confused, but he did his best to interpret. As he did, and all at once, Meetuku's eyes opened wide with wonder. He began to speak quickly.

"He asks, do you truly believe that magic brought you here? We Ticuna always learned that those who do not live in the Amazon do not believe in magic," Pepe interpreted.

Mary wasn't sure what to say.

"I guess it could have been magic, I really don't know. One moment we were far away, then we touched this object. It was a little a globe that showed the surface of the earth. Next, we were high above the earth, coming in closer to the Amazon. Then, before we knew what was happening, we were really here, in the rainforest."

It sounded foolish to Mary as she said it all. She wondered

what Meetuku and the others must be thinking. She hoped they wouldn't think she'd gone crazy.

But Meetuku didn't seem to think so at all. He took her words seriously, and his entire appearance changed. Looking like a prophet or great teacher, he began to explain in a passionate and eloquent tone. Mary listened closely as Pepe translated.

"We, the Ticuna," Meetuku declared, "still believe in magic. Even if others have forgotten, we live in the Amazon, and the Amazon will not let us forget. She is powerful with magic, and does many things to demonstrate her magic to us each day. Magic can come from the earth. Magic can come from the water. But the most powerful magic of all comes from the sky. It is the sky which is higher than us all, and looks down on us from afar. The sky gives us rain, bringing water to the land. This water brings us the river and all of its life. It brings us these tall trees, and all of their life. The powerful sky loves the Amazon, and brings her life each day. Where there is more life, there is more magic. When we have more magic, we have more life."

As Meetuku came to a pause in his sermon, everything was quiet. Mary tried to make sense of what he was saying. She wondered what this had to do with them. As if reading her mind, Meetuku continued.

"You came from the sky. You say you came by ways that you cannot understand. But we understand. If the sky brought you to the Amazon, then it is because you must also bring life to the Amazon."

A powerful, unexpected feeling came over Mary. She thought of all those times when she felt pulled to the Amazon. She assumed it was just a desire for adventure. Was it possible that it was actually some unseen magical force that wanted her here?

"You mean we came to do something for the rainforest?" Helen asked.

"Perhaps you have already done something for the rainforest," came the answer. "Many times, it is by small means that great things come to pass. Or perhaps you still have something to do, or many things to do. I cannot say. You must discover that for yourselves."

"So what does that mean?" Ike asked, with a hint of concern. "Does it mean that we can't go home?"

Meetuku's seriousness melted away, as he laughed after Pepe translated Ike's misgiving.

"Certainly you can home," he answered. "Everyone belongs in their home, even if we leave it for a time. If the magic needs to you to do something, it will be done. We cannot force when or how it will happen. All will be as it should."

Ike looked somewhat relieved.

Mary wanted to ask if the Ticuna could help them get home, but she didn't want to seem apathetic to the deep beliefs that Meetuku had just shared.

"Meetuku, we're very grateful for all of your help. And even though I don't know much about the Amazon or its magic, I want to do whatever the rainforest brought us here to do. But we're also very worried about our families. They don't know we're here," Mary explained.

After Pepe interpreted her words, Meetuku turned to Taremuku and Wueku. As Meetuku conversed with them, the old woman approached Mary. Thus far, she'd remained silent. She put her hand on Mary's shoulder and gave her a warm smile. She didn't speak, but Mary felt a sense of honor and respect in her presence.

After finishing their conversation with the Elder, Taremuku and Wueku gave a nod, and turned to leave.

"Taremuku and Wueku are my older brothers," Pepe explained. "Meetuku has asked them to prepare boats so that we can take you to Puerto Nariño, the nearest large village. There we can find a way to contact your family."

Mary couldn't help herself. She was so full of joy and gratitude that she threw her arms around Meetuku. A bit startled, the Elder patted her on the back and began to laugh. Helen jumped in the air, showing her excitement, and hugged the old woman. Ike tried to conceal his own obvious glee, casually offering his hand for Pepe to shake.

For the first time, the woman spoke, looking directly at Mary.

"This is Iatuna, grandmother to our entire village. She is the wisest among us in understanding the secrets and the magic of the Amazon. She can feel strong magic in each of you. She says that you are only at the beginning of a long journey, but that you will use your magic to change the world for the better," Pepe interpreted.

Everyone stood silently. Iatuna nodded slowly. A powerful feeling came from her, and Mary felt herself blush. She'd never believed in magic before. But Mary felt something, a sort of energy, coming from Iatuna. It was a sacred moment.

"Thank you again," Mary finally said to her new friends, as the magic of the moment slowly faded away. "You've saved our lives, and I hope that someday I can help pay you back. I hope that we can do whatever we're supposed to do here."

"I know you will, Mary," said Iatuna.

Even though she spoke in the Ticuna language, Mary understood her without interpretation. At this point, it didn't even surprise her.

I know you will.

CHAPTER SIXTEEN

The Guardians of the Amazon

Mary, Helen, and Ike spent another night in the Ticuna village. They were given the royal treatment, with a big dinner of barbecued fish and more fruit than they could eat in a lifetime. The Ticuna even put on a performance. Meetuku made sure that Mary understood that his was not a tribe that performed for tourists. This was a special honor for them as guests.

The Ticuna stood in a line, dancing and singing to the sound of drums and pipes. They wore beautifully colored macaw feathers, shining in their blues, reds, and yellows. Some wore wooden masks, carved or decorated with small stones, leaves, and feathers.

Mary and Helen clapped along, and were quickly invited to join in the dance. Excitedly, they both jumped up and danced along. Ike was invited to join too, and though he tried to protest, he eventually stood and danced, clearly having the time of his life.

When they'd danced so much they couldn't stand anymore, people began to file off to their homes. Most said goodbye to Mary, knowing they wouldn't see her the next morning. She hugged them all, feeling like they were family.

For the second night in a row, Mary enjoyed a comfortable sleep on a hammock. Pepe explained how the Ticuna didn't usually sleep in the hammocks at night, and typically used them for resting during the day. But Mary and the others wanted to sleep with the canopy of the trees as their roof, and the Ticuna consented. Kindly, they brought out mosquito netting and covered the hammocks, allowing Mary to enjoy a bug-free night.

Mary felt she'd hardly closed her eyes when someone lightly shook her awake. Pepe stood over her, with the first light of morning filtering through the trees.

"Time to leave," he said. "Our boats do not have motors, and it will take us many hours to get to Puerto Nariño."

Mary's sleepiness was quickly overcome by anticipation for the journey. She made her way to the edge of the river, where two large canoes waited, each stocked and ready for the trip. There was plenty of fish and fruit to feed them throughout the day.

Both Meetuku and Iatuna stood at the bank of the river, waiting to say their goodbyes. The aged leaders of the village wished them well, and Iatuna offered a sort of prayer for their journey. Mary embraced her hosts one last time, then boarded one of the boats, along with Wueku and Pepe. Helen and Ike joined Taremuku in the second canoe.

Within moments, both boats were pushed into the current, and they were on their way. Mary waved at Meetuku and Iatuna until her boat turned a corner in the river, and the village was out of sight.

Pepe and Wueku rowed Mary's boat, while Taremuku and Helen rowed in the second. Helen seemed to take naturally to the task. At first Mary felt that she should contribute in some way, not wanting to just sit while her hosts did all of the hard work.

"Do not worry, Mary," Pepe assured her. "We are used to these boats, and rowing is easy and natural to us. Just sit and enjoy the Amazon."

Mary settled into the canoe. Everything about the early morning Amazon was alive and magical. Birds flew above, or perched in trees nearby. Turtles and caimans climbed onto the banks to enjoy the first rays of sunlight. Mary watched an anaconda nimbly slither over a log and into the water.

After an hour or so of steadily gliding over the surface of the river, the current picked up. Pepe and Wueku no longer put much effort into rowing, instead using the oars to simply steer. Mary wondered, with no small measure of guilt, how long it would take for these small boats to return to the Ticuna village while going against the current.

The river grew wider, and Mary spotted other boats for the first time. Several of the boatmen stared in confusion at the strange collection of passengers in the Ticuna canoes.

"They wonder who you are," Pepe said with a laugh. "Within a few hours, every village within one hundred kilometers will hear about you."

Mary spent the next hour asking Pepe question after question about life in the Amazon. She had many, but he didn't seem to mind. She could feel how much the magical place meant to him.

"You really love this place, don't you?" she asked.

"Well of course!" Pepe exclaimed. "It is my home."

"What do you think will happen to the rainforest?" she questioned. "In school, we've learned a lot about how it's in danger."

Pepe let out a long sigh.

"It is true what you have learned, and a very sad thing. There are many, even some of our own people, who are destroying this place. Logging companies cut down the trees, ranchers destroy the land, and poachers make money by killing endangered species," Pepe explained.

"What can we do to stop it?" Mary wondered aloud.

"Unfortunately, not much. It would be easier if there were more of us. Then we could stand together and have greater influence. But year by year my people grow fewer and fewer. Life outside the rainforest has much to offer. Many leave to make a living, but when they leave the Amazon, the Amazon leaves them, and they never return."

It sounded sad and depressing. Mary understood that the world outside of the Amazon offered a lot of modern conveniences. But how could someone who grew up in this place turn away and leave it forever?

"But," Pepe then interjected, breaking the depressive silence with a tone of hope, "I plan to spend my life doing whatever is possible to change this. The solution is to build a bridge."

"A bridge? Over the river?" Mary asked, confused.

"Not a bridge between two riverbanks. A bridge of communication between our people and the outside world. I believe that the more people there are who understand what the Amazon means to us, the more we can find support to protect it," Pepe said.

Mary found herself wishing she could somehow help Pepe in his quest. She sat back, pondering about what she could do. As she stared at the beauty around her, Mary wondered how much of it would be lost if things didn't change.

Something caught her eye and took her attention away from these thoughts. Scanning the water, Mary thought she saw something move among the logs and floating debris. It was large and gray, yet only visible for a split second before submerging. A big fish, maybe?

Mary saw it again. But as before, it was gone almost as soon as it appeared, leaving only a slight spray of water. What seemed like several minutes passed, with only ripples visible in the current.

Then it appeared again. Only instead of gray, this time it looked pink.

I must be seeing things, Mary thought.

As soon as the thought crossed her mind, she saw both the pink something and the gray something make yet another brief appearance. Whatever was out there, there were two of them. And they were incredibly close to the canoe.

"Pepe, what are those things swimming near us in the water?" Mary asked, a bit concerned.

Pepe had been focused on avoiding logs, and hadn't seen

anything. He asked Wueku, but before his brother could answer, in a spray of water, one of the things leapt from the river. It shot several feet into the air, before splashing down next to Mary. It was large and pink, with shiny, smooth skin. In surprise, Mary jumped back, nearly causing the narrow boat to capsize.

Pepe laughed as he steadied the canoe. The thing jumped out of the water again, and this time was immediately followed by its gray companion.

"What are they?" Helen called from the other boat.

Mary, still recovering from the initial shock, suddenly realized what she was seeing.

"They're Amazon River Dolphins!" she declared, no longer frightened.

"I have seen them many times, but never so close to the boat like this. Usually they stay far from humans. They must like you, Mary," said Pepe.

Mary inched over to the side of the canoe for a better look. She moved slowly, not wanting to startle the dolphins. Peering into the water, Mary could see the pink dolphin, swimming just below the surface.

"Wow!" she whispered in amazement.

It slowly rose to the surface, to where Mary could see its entire body as it swam along. The dolphin's eye gazed directly at her, never moving away.

"Truly, Iatuna was right about you!" Pepe proclaimed. "Only the most magical can commune with the river guardians."

"They're beautiful!" Mary said. "What else can you tell me about them?"

Just as the dolphin kept its eye on Mary, she fixed her own gaze on the pink swimming mammal. It matched the speed of the canoe as it swam.

"Many in the Amazon fear them," Pepe explained. "We believe that if you kill one, you will suffer nightmares for the rest of your life. There are legends of dolphins who change into men. They come among us and choose our beautiful women to be their wives. When a young woman disappears and is never seen again, her family often claims she was taken by a dolphin."

"Do you believe any of that?" asked Mary.

"I am not sure," Pepe admitted. "Part of me does not believe, but then again, these stories and legends are part of the culture of my people."

Suddenly Pepe laughed.

"But there are many who truly do believe, like my younger sister. Once I found her sitting on the river bank, singing to the water. She hoped a handsome dolphin would come and choose her. But she is still with us, so I guess she is not their type."

Mary laughed and continued to watch the dolphin in amazement.

Suddenly, Wueku sat stiffly upright, hissing out words in an angry tone. Wondering what was causing his reaction, Mary turned her gaze from the dolphin to see a fancy-looking speed boat approaching. It slowed as it got closer. When she turned back to the dolphin, it had vanished.

A single person manned the boat, and he definitely wasn't from the Amazon.

"G'day, there!" the captain said in a strong Australian accent.

He was probably about forty years old, and wore fancy sunglasses and a wide-brimmed hat. His skin was deeply tanned, and he had a rifle slung over his shoulder. Wueku spat out what sounded like a string of curses in the man's direction.

"Easy there, mate," the Australian boatman replied. "I don't speak any of your Indian gibberish. I just saw the dolphins jumping so close to your boat, and I had to see with my own eyes. How'd you get 'em to do that? Eh, you don't even understand me, do you?"

"We understand you fine," Pepe answered, "and we have

done nothing to make the dolphins come close to us. They have chosen to do this on their own."

"Are you fair dinkum?" the Australian said in surprise. "I suppose I've just about seen everything. River dolphins swimming with boats. Indians speaking English. Good on you, mate!"

Pepe seemed irritated, and didn't reply.

"Tell me," the Australian continued, ignoring the scowls on the faces of the Ticuna, "have you seen any more of the dolphins about? I've been out fishing all day, and they're always good at leading me to a big catch!"

"I have seen no other dolphins," Pepe said curtly to the boatman.

The Australian glanced over at Mary for the first time.

"We'll I'll be, the little sheila doesn't look like she's from around these parts. Do you speak English there too, girly?" he asked, locking eyes with Mary.

Mary felt a shiver run down her spine.

"I do," she said, timidly. "We're guests of our friends."

"Is that right?" the Australian replied. "And where are your parents?"

Mary looked into the man's boat as she thought about how to answer. She gasped as she noticed something bloody and covered with a tarp.

"We're going to meet them now," she said, trying not to be obvious about what she'd seen.

"And where might they be?" the man pressed.

Mary hardly heard him. She felt a sinking pit in her stomach as she stared at the tarp-covered thing in his boat. She had to know. Ignoring his question, she countered with one of her own.

"What's that in your boat?"

The boatman glanced at tarp, and quickly covered what looked like a pink-colored fin.

"Oh, that? Just the fish I've pulled in so far today," he answered, shifting nervously.

The sickening feeling made Mary feel like she was about to faint. That certainly hadn't looked like a fish. She didn't see much, but there was no mistaking that rosy pink color.

"Well girly, you be careful. The Amazon's a dangerous place," the man said, hurriedly. "I reckon it's time for me to shove off."

Before Mary could say another word, the Australian hit the throttle and sped away. As his boat picked up speed and cruised down the river, Wueku launched another volley of Ticuna expletives in the man's direction. The Australian's motor caused a powerful wake in the river, and their canoe rocked back and forth.

As soon as the man was out of sight, Mary turned to Pepe, tears already in her eyes.

"Was that what I thought it was?" she cried out.

"Yes, I am afraid so," Pepe replied. "I told you there are poachers here who are destroying what is most sacred to us."

"But why would he kill a dolphin?" Mary asked, genuinely perplexed. "Do people eat them?"

"No," Pepe answered sullenly. "They are cut to pieces and used as bait to catch fish."

Mary couldn't believe it. Who would kill one of these majestic creatures only to use them as fish bait?

Wueku exchanged a rapid and heated conversation with Pepe.

"Wueku believes this is the same poacher who has been killing jaguars near our home. In fact, Wueku and Taremuku had been tracking an injured jaguar when they found you, cornered by the starving animal. This poacher set snares throughout the jungle in an attempt to catch or injure jaguars and make them easier to hunt," Pepe interpreted.

Mary remembered the jaguar's bloody paw. It had been desperate.

"You mean he's killing dolphins *and* jaguars?" she said, even more shocked. "That's terrible! What can we can do to stop him?"

"We can inform the authorities when we arrive in Puerto Nariño," Pepe suggested. "Unfortunately, professional poachers like this man are good at being hard to catch."

Mary cried as she thought about all that she'd just seen.

"Pepe, do you really believe the rainforest is magical?" Mary asked, sniffling.

"It is hard for me to say. In my school, they tell me that there is no magic, only superstition. But our wisest elders like Meetuku and Iatuna believe, and they have seen many things. They have lived longer than my teacher, and I think they understand these things better," Pepe said.

Mary thought about the globe. Did magic make it work? Or was there some rational scientific explanation? Or is that what magic was—science that was just beyond human ability to understand?

Pepe continued, "for instance, Iatuna once told me that the dolphins are the guardians of the Amazon. As long as they are still here, the Amazon will be here. As long as the Amazon is here, the forests will remain. And as long as there are forests and trees, my people will live here. It is all part of the great magic that connects all living things."

"And if the dolphins disappear?" Mary asked.

"Then some of that magic will leave from the river. If magic leaves from the river, it will then leave the forest. If we are all connected, then it leads us closer to the end of my people."

He sounded genuinely sad.

"Are you afraid that will happen?" Mary asked.

"Our elders say that the rivers were once filled with dolphins. Now, there are fewer and fewer. And not only poachers cause the problems. Many of them die from pollution and other things. Even if the dolphins are not magic, they are a part of this place. If they go, a piece of the soul of the Amazon is gone too. I am afraid of that."

Mary sat in silence for a moment as she contemplated Pepe's words.

"Now I understand why you want to build your bridge," she said.

"Yes," he replied. "I want to do all I can to protect my home. It is who I am. Without the dolphins, or without the Amazon, or without the rainforest, I will lose part of who I am."

Pepe spoke with conviction. He understood his life's work.

"I want to help you," Mary offered. "I believe that this place really is full of magic. I don't know how to explain it, but I can feel it. I believe it, Pepe, and I'll do whatever I can to help you protect this place from people like that poacher."

Pepe smiled.

"Meetuku teaches that we are all small," he said. "But from small things come great things. Every tall tree in the rainforest begins as a tiny seed. Even this river begins as small drops of water. As many small drops join, they become the mighty Amazon."

"I like that," Mary reflected. "I know I'm small, but if I do what I can, I'll become part of something great."

"If I can build my bridge, maybe I can convince others to join me. You, Mary, can build your own bridges. Your magic will help. It is clear that the guardians of the river believe you have a purpose," said Pepe, gesturing to the dolphins, which had returned and resumed following the canoe. "They must know that you will do something important. I will help them protect you, so you can do these great things."

Pepe's words opened up so many new ideas for Mary. "Great things" echoed in her head. She glanced again at the dolphins swimming alongside the canoe. She couldn't let them down. Not the dolphins, and not the Ticuna. Mary would discover what she was meant to do. Little by little, the magic of the Amazon was opening a new world of understanding right before her eyes.

CHAPTER SEVENTEEN

Puerto Nariño

After several hours on the river, Mary saw a settlement on the banks up ahead.

"Puerto Nariño," Pepe announced, pointing to the village.

The entire town was small enough that Mary could see from one end to the other. In the middle was a town square, with sidewalks leading from that central point to all the different parts of the community. Little houses lined the narrow streets.

"It's so small!" Helen said in surprise, as the two canoes pulled alongside one another.

"Maybe it is not Miami, but it is one of the largest Ticuna villages in the Amazon," Pepe said.

"Puerto Nariño's a Ticuna village?" Mary asked.

"Not everybody is of the Ticuna, but most are. More than six thousand in one village. Here, the people are much more connected to the outside world, but many do not forget where they come from. It is a good bridge." Pepe explained.

"But how do you get anywhere?" Ike asked. "The town's completely surrounded by the rainforest on all sides. I don't see any cars or roads leading out."

"You are sitting on the only road," Pepe laughed. "Who needs highways when the largest river in the world takes you wherever you need? Besides, Puerto Nariño does not allow any cars or motorcycles. It is in their laws."

"None at all?" Helen asked.

"Well," Pepe said, "there is a small ambulance. But it is rarely used, and is mostly for tourists to look at. The village has many laws about pollution, recycling, and energy saving."

Mary was fascinated. Puerto Nariño looked so organized and clean. The massive green trees of the rainforest, which surrounded the community on all sides, gave the impression that the town was a fortress with a mighty wall protecting it.

Pepe steered their canoe toward one of the docks. The two dolphin guards finally parted and left them for the opposite side of the river. As they came up to the dock, Pepe jumped out and pulled the canoe away from other boats. Taremuku did the same. They were approached by another young man, and after a quick conversation in Ticuna, were shown where they could pull the boats onto land.

Once the canoes were beached, Pepe and Taremuku held out hands to help Mary, Helen and Ike climb onto dry land. They'd been sitting for hours, and it felt wonderful to Mary to stretch her legs again.

"Follow me," Pepe said. "We will see if the mayor is in his office. He will certainly want to meet you."

Taremuku and Wueku stayed behind to take care of the canoes, while Pepe led Mary, Helen, and Ike up the sloping pathway and into the town. It didn't take long until they'd reached the small square in the town's center. The largest building was a two-story structure made from bricks painted bright yellow. The Colombian flag flapped in the breeze atop a tall flagpole.

Pepe led them into the building, and knocked on the first door they came to. A voice yelled from inside, and Pepe opened the door, gesturing for the group to enter.

A somewhat stout, middle-aged man in a short-sleeved white collared shirt sat at a desk. Various papers were strewn in front of him, and he peered through his glasses at a newspaper. He looked up at his visitors, and smiled as he recognized Pepe. He stood and shook hands with Pepe as the two chatted for a moment in Ticuna.

"Hello and welcome friends," said the man in heavily-accented English as he turned to his foreign visitors. "You welcome my village. Please make my home you home!"

"Señor Peñuela is the mayor of Puerto Nariño, and one of the great representatives for the Ticuna in Colombia," Pepe said. "I have told him of your situation, and he is ready to help you."

The mayor pulled out an old telephone with a rotary dial.

"Please," he said, nodding. "Phone who you like."

After the mayor showed them how to make an international call, Mary dialed the only phone number she had memorized—that of her own home. She'd never made a call on a rotary telephone before. The string of numbers seemed they'd never end.

Mary finally finished dialing, and held the receiver close to her ear. Would it even work? Eventually, the old phone rang four times before somebody picked up on the other end.

"Hello?" said Mary's mother, through heavy static.

"Mom!" Mary cried out.

Mary expected Mom to scream in joy or astonishment. Instead, all she heard was silence.

"Mom, it's me, Mary!" she tried again.

"Hello? Is someone there?" said Mom's voice, the connection making it sound like she was underwater.

Even with the bad connection, Mom sounded tired and hollow. Mary imagined how Mom must be going through torture not knowing where her children were, and whether or not they were okay. And now, with proof that they were fine pressed against her ear, technology refused to give her the news she so desperately needed. Mary felt anxiety steadily growing within her.

"Yes Mom, it's me, Mary. I'm okay and Ike and Helen are with me, but we need—"

"Whoever it is, I can't hear anything," Mom said in a weak, exasperated voice.

Mary groaned in frustration. The joyful emotion of hearing her mother's voice was gone, replaced by irritation.

"Mom, listen closely, we need—"

With a sudden click, the line went dead. Mom was gone.

"It didn't work. She couldn't hear me," Mary complained.

She tried to dial the number again. Once more, Mary went through the tedious succession of numbers. This time, it didn't even ring. Instead, it gave a recorded error message in Spanish.

Mary handed the receiver to Mayor Peñuela, shaking her head.

"Aww, man!" Ike said, disheartened. "How are we supposed to get home now?"

"Yeah, what are we going to do?" Helen asked.

Mary couldn't help but think about all that Meetuku and Iatuna had said about the magic of the rainforest, and how they'd come here for a reason. Was something trying to keep them from contacting home? If so, then Mary wished it would stop. After hearing her Mom's voice, and knowing that she was in pain, all Mary wanted right now was to help her.

"I don't know," Mary said. "I guess we'll just have to try again later?"

"What about email?" Pepe suggested.

All three kids turned to Pepe with surprised looks on their faces.

Of course! Mary thought. *Why didn't I think of that?*

She was embarrassed, realizing she'd assumed that life in the Amazon must surely be too primitive for more modern technology.

"You have internet here?" Ike said, clearly not at all embarrassed for having the same thought.

"Of course," Pepe replied with a sly grin. "We may be in the Amazon, but this is still the twenty-first century. Without the internet, how would I keep in touch with my friends on Facebook?"

Pepe explained everything to the mayor, who nodded and

led them into the next room. An older-looking computer sat on a desk. After switching it on, Mayor Peñuela gestured for Mary to take the chair.

It took a moment for the computer to fully load, but once it did, Mary had no trouble logging into her personal email account. She clicked to compose a new message. She was just about to start typing, when she realized something.

"I've never emailed my parents before," she said. "I only use my email for school."

Dad was always a big stickler about spending too much time behind the computer screen, and was constantly lecturing the kids about how the internet and social media were depriving their generation of social skills.

"How about you, Helen, do you know your parents' email addresses?" Ike asked.

"Not exactly," Helen confessed. "I always just text with mine. Email's for old people."

Mary, realizing this was going to be harder than it seemed, dropped her head on the keyboard in exasperation.

Just then, the old rotary phone in the next room began to ring. She listened as Mayor Peñuela answered, and soon his footsteps approached from the next room.

The mayor looked completely dumfounded.

"For you," he said.

CHAPTER EIGHTEEN

The Mysterious Caller

Mary was just as surprised as the mayor. She crossed into the other room and picked up the phone.

"Hello?" she said, unsure of what to expect.

"Mary! It's you!" said Grandpa from the other end.

"Grandpa!" Mary yelled in complete bewilderment. "How'd you know where we were?"

"Mary, the minute I saw the surveillance video of you kids disappearing with the globe, I knew you could be anywhere. I figured you'd be smart enough to call home at the first possible chance. I asked an old friend from the phone company to help track any out-of-area calls to your parents' home," he explained. "Right after your call came in, he let me know, and was able to connect me directly to you."

"Grandpa, you're a genius!" Mary exclaimed, overwhelmed with joy.

"More like a fool," Grandpa said, sounding ashamed. "I should've never hidden such a dangerous object in the museum. It's been there for more than thirty years, and I assumed nobody would ever find it."

"Grandpa, we're the ones who were touching your things without asking," Mary confessed. "We should be apologizing to you."

"Nonsense!" Grandpa retorted. "There's nothing wrong with being curious. That's what being a kid—especially a Tucker kid—is all about."

"Grandpa?"

"Yes, dear?"

"We need help. How can we get home?"

Grandpa chuckled.

"Mary, I can help you get home before dinner."

"What?" Mary said, incredulously. "How's that even possible? Grandpa, we're in the Amazon!"

"I know that, dear," said Grandpa, still laughing. "My friend at the phone company told me. I should have known that you'd somehow find your way there, given that it's where you wanted to go more than anyplace else."

"But Grandpa, don't you see? It'll probably take us days to even get to a city with an airport, let alone fly home," she protested.

"Now, Mary," Grandpa said patiently, "I'm a little surprised that you haven't figured it out yet on your own. If you used the globe to get there, why don't you just use it to come back?"

Mary was completely confused. She also felt a sharp pang of guilt. Grandpa's words reminded her how she'd let the globe fall into the janitor's hands.

"Grandpa, what are you talking about? As soon as we got to the rainforest, we couldn't find the globe anywhere. We didn't know it would bring us here. But it was gone when we arrived. We realized that it must have stayed at the warehouse," she explained.

Mary started crying.

"Grandpa, we lost it," she said. "The janitor came to the warehouse and tried to steal it from us, and I wanted to keep him from getting it. Instead, I accidently put it right in his hands."

Mary broke down even more.

"Oh, Mary, don't cry," Grandpa said. "I saw the janitor on the security video. It was a brave thing that you did. I have a bad feeling that I know exactly who he is too. If I'm right, it's a man named Anatoly. I crossed paths with him many years ago, and he tried to steal the globe then. I never imagined he'd track me down."

"Grandpa, I'm so sorry. Now he has the globe, and it's all my fault!" Mary said, her tears now coming in torrents.

"Hush now, child," Grandpa said in an extra soothing tone. "Don't waste your tears. He most definitely does *not* have the globe."

"He doesn't?" Mary said, perking up in surprise. "How do you know?"

"Because I've used that globe thousands of times to travel all over the world. I can promise you that when you use it to travel, it travels with you," Grandpa explained.

Mary felt the weight of the revelation hit her like a freight train. On one hand, she was elated that the janitor didn't have it after all. Yet at the same time, she felt distraught. It meant that the globe was still missing somewhere deep in the rainforest.

"What?" said Mary with disbelief. "But we looked everywhere! We fell into a tree and I was knocked unconscious. I didn't have it when I woke up. When we finally got down, we looked all over the ground nearby, but we couldn't find it anywhere."

"Well, it has to be there somewhere. At least this explains

why you haven't already tried to use it to come back home," Grandpa said. "I should've never doubted my brilliant granddaughter. I'm so sorry you've been carrying that guilt with you for the past few days."

"I thought I'd let you down," she sniffled.

"And I was beginning to think something horrible had happened, like you taking yourselves to the middle of the ocean or something like that. I've been carrying my own guilt these last few days, and trust me, until you're home safe it's not going anywhere," Grandpa said.

"So, you're sure it came with us?" Mary asked. "We really did look hard for it."

"Mary, I know you've already been through a lot, but is there any way you could go back and search the area more? Maybe the globe was caught in the tree's branches?" Grandpa wondered.

Mary immediately began to think about what it would take for them to retrieve the globe. If it was stuck in the tree, then maybe, with the help of the Ticuna, they'd be able to find it.

"I think we could try," Mary said. "But it might take a few days. We're far away from where we landed originally. And what if we can't find it?" Mary asked.

"We'll find a way to get you home no matter what,"

Grandpa said. "But, Mary, I don't mean to be the bearer of bad news, but getting home through normal ways won't be a quick process. You're in another country, without a passport or any other documentation. I'll have to talk to lawyers, pay fines, and find other ways to prove who you are before you'll be able to leave. It could take weeks or even months to get it all figured out."

Mary hadn't thought about all of that. She'd never traveled before, but it made sense that there would be all sorts of legal problems with foreign kids just showing up in the Amazon. Mary didn't know what to say.

"But my girl, don't you worry. If that's what it takes, then I'll do it," he continued. "I'll come and get you myself if I have to. But if you can somehow find the globe, then you'd be home a lot faster."

Mary knew he was right.

"I'll do it Grandpa, but there's another thing I'm worried about."

"Yes, dear?" he replied.

"Is there a way you can help us let Mom and Dad know that we're okay? And Helen's parents too? When I called the connection was bad, and Mom couldn't hear me. I don't know their email addresses either," Mary explained.

"I'll talk to them again. I tried to tell them about the

globe, but they've been so distraught that they refused to listen to me. They thought that you kids going missing was driving me crazy, and that I was making up stories to cope."

Knowing Dad, Mary wasn't surprised.

"But maybe you could help make it more convincing," he continued. "You could send a message to the museum. I know your dad sees all of the general queries that people make through the museum's website. Maybe that will be enough to get him to believe me."

"That's a great idea!" Mary said, remembering how Dad frequently complained about the general museum query emails that were always forwarded directly to his personal account.

He wouldn't be complaining this time.

"Mary, I can't tell you how happy this makes me to hear your voice," Grandpa said. "And I know your parents will be so—"

Grandpa suddenly cut off in the middle of his sentence.

"Grandpa, are you still there?" Mary asked.

"Yes, I'm still here," he said, after a pause. "I just thought I heard something. Like somebody else breathing and listening in on our conversation."

The way Grandpa reacted made her skin prickle.

"I didn't hear anything," she said. "Maybe it's just static."

"I'm sorry, Mary," Grandpa said. "I'm just being paranoid. After seeing Anatoly hold you at gunpoint on that security video, I've been extra worried. He fled the museum soon after you disappeared, and hasn't been seen since. Your parents think he did something to you."

"Grandpa, do you think he's been looking for it all these years?" Mary asked.

"Could be. Sometimes greed does scary things to people," Grandpa said.

Now that she knew Anatoly didn't have the globe after all, Mary realized he'd still be looking for it. They were safe in the Amazon for now, but what about Grandpa and her parents? Were they in danger? It struck Mary that she needed to be very careful about what she said over the phone or put in an email.

"Grandpa," Mary said, "maybe we shouldn't talk about the you-know-what anymore."

"Mary, once again, I knew you had more brains than you'd ever need," Grandpa said.

"I'll try to find the … uh, find it," she corrected. "Hopefully it will only take a few days."

"And I'll start doing whatever I can to get you home as soon as possible, just in case you can't find it," Grandpa promised.

"Thank you!" Mary said, grateful for such a loving grandfather.

"Mary?" said Grandpa. "I'm so sorry you have to go through all of this. But I want you to know, that I wouldn't trust anybody else in the world more than you to succeed."

His words made Mary swell with pride, and fresh tears began to run down her cheeks.

"I love you, my girl. Get home soon," he said.

"I will. And I love you too."

CHAPTER NINETEEN

Rain

M ary was elated after talking to Grandpa. For the first time since coming to the rainforest, she felt nothing but confidence. Everything was going to turn out okay, even if finding the globe wouldn't be easy.

Before that could even happen, Mary needed to let her parents know that she was safe. On Grandpa's suggestion, she found the museum's website. Using the generic contact email, Mary wrote a message, deliberately keeping it short. Thinking of Anatoly and potential dangers, she didn't give details. Grandpa could fill her parents in on all the rest.

Dear Dad (Lewis Tucker),

This is Mary. I'm with Ike and Helen. We're all okay, but it's a long story. We'll be home as soon as we can. Talk to Grandpa, he'll explain everything. No matter how crazy it sounds, he's telling the truth. We love you and we'll see you soon. Please tell Mom and Helen's parents that we're okay.

Love, Mary

Satisfied, Mary turned off the computer and felt the burden lift from her shoulders. Hopefully, her note would be enough to help ease the anguish her parents were feeling.

The next step was to get back to the tree where they started. Mary was suddenly grateful to Ike for his insistence that they mark their path, despite her initial resistance to the idea. She was nervous, however, about asking Pepe, Taremuku, and Wueku to take them back upriver. They'd already done so much to help.

But Mary needn't have been worried. Her Ticuna friends not only eagerly agreed to take them back to find the tree, they promised to enlist other Ticuna to search the area for the globe. Mary didn't feel she'd ever be able to repay their kind hosts for all they'd done.

There was one problem. The weather had taken a turn for the worst. Only an hour after arriving in Puerto Nariño, the skies opened and began dumping water on the village in buckets.

"I think we will need to wait here until the rain stops," Pepe said reluctantly. "I am sorry, but it is too dangerous to try and face the river upstream with so much rain."

"It's alright," Mary conceded. "It'll take us a few days to get there anyway. Another day won't hurt."

Learning that they'd spend the night in Puerto Nariño, Mayor Peñuela rolled out the red carpet for his guests. Eager to be hospitable, he offered them a place to stay, completely free of charge. Under umbrellas provided by the mayor, they made their way to a small motel.

"You stay here all days you need," said the mayor with a wink.

Though small, the motel was clean and comfortable. After three nights in the wild, little things like a hot shower felt like amazing luxuries to Mary. Pepe, Taremuku, and Wueku left them at their quarters, opting to stay with cousins in town.

"Wow, this is almost like a vacation!" Ike said, kicking up his feet in front of the television.

Mary thought it wouldn't be such a bad thing if they had to wait for an extra day or two for the rain to stop. She got ready for bed, and as soon as the sun went down, had no problem falling asleep.

She awoke the next morning to more heavy rainfall. Apparently, the rainforest really didn't want her to leave. Mary hoped Dad had received her message. She thought about trying to write or call again, but decided against it when she remembered Anatoly. It was best to let Grandpa handle everything.

Pepe stopped by around mid-morning, confirming that the weather was still too rough to travel upriver. To pass the time, he offered to take them into the forest and show them around.

"Not a chance," Helen said, as Mary announced that Pepe was waiting outside. "There's no way that I'm going out in the rain!"

"Neither am I," Ike said. "Why be wet when you can sit in a dry motel room watching Latin American soap operas instead?"

"He makes an excellent point," Helen added.

"Alejandra, ¿qué estás haciendo?" Ike said, in his best imitation of the male actor on the TV screen.

"¡Déjame en paz!" said Helen, likewise imitating the woman.

Both Helen and Ike almost fell on the floor laughing at themselves.

Mary didn't find it funny. How could they waste their

opportunity to explore the rainforest with a native, and sit around instead watching TV? The whole thing felt sacrilegious to her. She marched over to the television, and switched it off.

"Hey! What gives?" Ike complained.

"I'm sorry," Mary said. "I know you might not be as into the rainforest as I am, but I'm not going to let you waste this chance while you just sit here watching stupid telenovelas! The Ticuna saved our lives, remember? You're both coming with me, and that's final!"

Mary had never seen Helen and Ike look so surprised. They started putting on their shoes without saying another word.

Mary and Helen pulled on Grandpa's raincoats, while Ike grabbed one of the borrowed umbrellas. They bustled outside, where Pepe stood waiting. He wasn't bothered by the rain at all. Water streamed down his face like a faucet.

"Are you ready to see how beautiful the forest can be when it rains?" he asked.

Together, they trudged across the wet grass toward the jungle's edge.

The world changed once they were beneath the tall trees. Despite the rain, things were as alive as ever. Streams of water trickled sporadically from the thick leaves above. Mary smiled as she became entranced by the familiar music of the heavy rainfall on the canopy coupled with the sounds of animals throughout the rainforest.

Pepe excitedly showed them every wonderful thing he could spot. With ease, he found animals, plants, and more that Mary would have never noticed.

These forests were his home, after all.

A whistling sounded in the distance. A bird, perhaps? Pepe answered by holding his hands against his lips, and perfectly imitating the sound.

Responding to the call, Taremuku and Wueku came strolling through the trees. They were wet from top to bottom. Wueku carried a basket full of fruit. He passed around a sort of small, wild mango, which was absolutely delicious.

Biting into his third mango, Taremuku pointed into the trees.

"Oh yes, there it is," Pepe said, pointing out a particular limb far above.

Mary only saw a clump of moss. Then it began to slowly move. She soon recognized that the moss was actually a tree sloth, methodically climbing along a limb.

"Aww, it's so cute!" Ike said, sarcastically.

"They do make good pets," Pepe said. "I had one as a child."

Mary enjoyed a few more hours in the rainforest, with her capable Ticuna guides pointing out every interesting thing they could find. They found leafcutter ants marching in a row over a log, each carrying a triangular piece of green leaf. They pointed out different edible fruits. There were tree frogs, lizards, monkeys—you name it. There was so much life in such a small area.

Mary was beginning to feel just as happy and at home in the rainforest as the Ticuna.

"Aren't you glad you didn't stay in the motel watching TV?" she asked Helen and Ike.

"Yeah, I've got to admit, it's pretty awesome out here," Helen replied.

"Well, I guess it depends on what was on TV … " Ike said, before quickly dodging the mango stone that Mary threw in his direction.

Ike slipped as he ducked, but came up laughing. He started to chase Mary, and soon they all joined it, running around the trees, laughing, and having a great time.

It could have lasted forever, but their fun was suddenly interrupted.

"Bang!"

CHAPTER TWENTY

The Poacher

The sound of the gun echoed among the trees. Taremuku, Wueku, and Pepe were on full alert, low to the ground, and whispering. Taremuku gestured for Mary to get down.

"What is it?" Mary asked.

"It can only be a poacher," he replied. "No hunting is allowed in this protected area."

Wueku looked angry, and argued in harsh whispers with Taremuku and Pepe.

"You guys can't be thinking of going after him," Helen said, guessing the topic of their heated discussion. "Whoever's out there has a gun!"

Pepe translated, and Wueku responded with passion.

"I know this is the same man who continues to destroy our home. The officials will never arrest him because he bribes them to look the other way. If we don't stop him, who will?"

Bang! Another gunshot rang out, this time closer.

Wueku gritted his teeth and made to run in the direction of the sound. Taremuku grabbed him, keeping him on the ground.

"Wait!" Mary said. "Maybe there's another way? Maybe we can help?"

"How?" Pepe asked. "You do not have weapons either."

"He won't think American children in the forest are a threat. Maybe we can use that to our advantage?"

The group gathered around, while Mary whispered a plan.

"Mary, you are clever indeed," Pepe said. "I would have never thought of such a thing."

"Are you sure about this?" Helen asked.

Mary wasn't sure at all. She was trembling just thinking about it. But she understood how Wueku felt. Images of a dead dolphin flashed before her eyes. She had to do something. It was as if the magic of the rainforest was willing her to do something.

"Yes," she said. "But we'll all need to do our part. Are you with me?"

"I'm in if you are," said Helen resolutely.

"Me too," said Ike, looking surprisingly eager.

Their plan in place, the children began walking cautiously toward the gunfire.

"Hello? Is anybody out there? We need your help! Help!" they all cried out.

The three of them moved as a group, doing their best to make sure the poacher heard them before he saw them.

Mary turned to look for her Ticuna companions. Their job was to stay out of sight. Given that Mary couldn't see any trace of them, they were doing an excellent job of that.

"Hello?" she continued to cry out. "Is anybody there?"

"Over here!" came the reply at last.

There was no mistaking that strong Australian accent.

"Where are you?" Mary called.

Back and forth they communicated, until she could finally see the poacher ahead, standing in the trees.

This was it. It was now or never. Mary, Ike, and Helen all ran toward the man.

"Thank goodness!" Mary cried out, trying her hardest to sound desperate. "We've been lost in the forest for hours!"

"What the devil's all this about?" the Australian man said, a look of absolute consternation crossing his face. "What are you three doing out 'ere alone?"

"We were staying in Puerto Nariño," Mary whimpered. "We decided we'd go for a walk in the rainforest this morning, but we got lost. We've been wandering around for hours trying to get back. We thought we'd be lost forever, until we heard the gun. Are you with the search party?"

The man shuffled nervously on his feet.

"Well, uh, no. Not exactly," he said. "I was just out for a walk m'self."

"Can you help us?" Helen asked. "Can we go back to the town with you? Please?"

The man looked more and more uncomfortable.

"I, uh, I didn't come from the town," he explained. "The name's Colin, and I'm just a visitor in these parts too, you see. My boat's tucked into a little lagoon not far from here, and I wasn't planning on going back by way of the town."

Yeah, right, Mary thought.

He was just afraid of being recognized.

"Oh no!" she said, sounding distraught. "How are we supposed to get back?"

She was really getting into the acting. She actually felt real tears forming.

"Oh come now, little sheila," Colin said. "There's no need to cry. I can at least take you to the water's edge and maybe a passing boat can take you to where you need to be."

Mary sniffled, trying to sound consoled.

"Thank you," she said.

Mary quickly glanced at Ike, cuing him to his turn.

"That's a cool gun," he said to Colin. "Are you a real hunter?"

"Oh, this thing?" the poacher said, glancing at his rifle. "I'm not actually hunting, you see. It's illegal here, after all. I was just carrying it for protection against jaguars and the like. I was just doing a little bit of target practice, that's all."

Colin sounded convincing. He'd likely used this story before to get out of trouble.

"I'll bet you're a really good shot. I wish I knew how to shoot a gun," Ike said. "Then I wouldn't have to worry about jaguars either."

The man smiled, obviously taking a liking to Ike. Mary couldn't help but be impressed with how genuine her little brother sounded.

"I'm not so bad with it," Colin boasted. "Here, watch this. Do you see that branch in that tree down yonder?"

"Yeah," Ike said. "Can you hit it? All the way from here?"

"You might want to plug your ears," Colin cautioned.

Without another word, the poacher pulled the gun to his shoulder, took careful aim, and fired. The weapon roared, and the branch splintered from the tree.

"That's awesome!" Ike said. "I wish I could do that."

The poacher smiled widely.

"You seem like a good young bloke. How'd you like to try it out?" Colin offered.

"Really? You mean it?" Ike said, acting completely surprised.

"Why not?" Colin replied. "Give 'er a try."

And with that, the man handed the long rifle to Ike.

"Wow!" Ike said, holding the gun in his hands and looking at it with fascination. "I've never held a real gun before. How do I shoot it?"

"Here, I'll show you," Colin said. "It's not all that difficult. Even a child can learn."

The poacher explained how to hold the gun, with stock tightly against the shoulder. He described how to align the spotting scope with the target.

The gun looked way too big in Ike's hands, but he was determined as he peered through the scope into the forest.

"Can I fire?" he asked, his voice full of eager anticipation.

"Okay, mate," Colin answered. "Only be careful. She's got a bit of a kick."

"Don't worry. I'm going to hit that big tree!" Ike said.

He squeezed the trigger, and the gun went off with a deafening bang. Immediately, Ike fell backward, the kick of the rifle taking him clean off his feet.

"Oh, mate, are you alright?" Colin asked in alarm.

Ike was fine, as he sat laughing on the ground.

"That was so cool! I didn't realize it'd be so strong."

"Yeah, nice shot clumsy," Helen said, laughing at Ike. "I think the tree doesn't have anything to worry about if you're shooting."

"You've got be careful, mate. Like I said, she carries a kick alright," Colin said. "Always be ready for that."

"Can I try it one more time?" Ike asked, standing and aiming the gun again.

"Well, I don't know about that," the poacher replied, as he reached for his gun.

"Please, only once more? I promise that's all. I just want to see if I can stay up."

Colin seemed more nervous than ever, perhaps rethinking the wisdom of letting a nine-year-old fire his gun in the first place.

"Alright, mate," he relented. "One last time."

"I'll drill that tree this time for sure!"

Once again, Ike aimed, standing with one foot staggered behind him, determined not to lose his balance this time.

"Ready!" he cried. "Aim … "

Instead of saying "fire," Ike dropped the weapon from his

shoulder. With the barrel pointed downward, he turned and started running as quickly as his short legs would carry him. He disappeared into the forest, the large gun still in his hands.

"Hey kid, what're you doin'?" Colin said, frantic as he watched his weapon disappear.

The Australian started to chase after Ike. Quicker than lightning, Helen was in front of him. She dropped to her hands and knees, blocking his path.

Crying out in surprise, the poacher's legs were taken out from under him. Carried by his own momentum, he tumbled through the air, end over end, before hitting the ground in a heap.

"Strewth, that hurt!" Colin cursed in pain, as he rolled in the dirt.

Mary was standing over him.

"I'm sorry, but you're under arrest," she said. "Poaching is illegal."

"What?" Colin said, confused. "You're arresting me?"

At first, a smile crossed his face, showing his amusement with the situation. His smile quickly faded when three native Amazonian men stepped up behind her.

"No, sir," Pepe corrected. "*We* are arresting you."

CHAPTER TWENTY-ONE

After the Hunt

The smile on Mary's face refused to disappear as they marched Colin back to Puerto Nariño. Taremuku had fashioned a rope out of long fibers he stripped from a plant, and tied the poacher's hands behind his back. Pepe and Ike took Colin's keys and went to retrieve his boat.

"You were amazing!" Helen said as they walked back to the town. "You should be an actress. I can't believe you were able to come up with that idea so quickly!"

"Not as amazing as you," Mary complimented back. "You were so fast! He never saw you coming."

"I'm telling you, girls, you got the wrong guy!" Colin protested as he marched along. "I'm no poacher! I'm just a normal bloke, trying to make ends meet in the world."

Wueku shot a few angry words in Ticuna and jabbed the man in the back with the barrel of his own hunting rifle.

"Alright, mate, alright," Colin said. "I'll shut it."

It took a good twenty minutes before they were back in Puerto Nariño. The group was quite a sight as they emerged from the trees. Ike and Pepe were already there, waiting with Mayor Peñuela and the village police officer. On top of that, a small crowd of curious onlookers had gathered.

The policeman cut the makeshift rope from the poacher's hands, only to replace it with steel handcuffs. Wueku relinquished the rifle to the policeman, who then led the poacher through the crowd and into the village.

Mayor Peñuela looked as happy as a man who'd just won the lottery.

"Thank you friends!" he said. "You help the Amazon, and stop this bad man."

"What's going to happen to him?" Helen asked.

"Puerto Nariño has a small jail," Pepe explained. "The town will hold him there for now. We have already contacted the authorities. They will come in the next few days to pick him up."

Pepe chuckled, as if realizing something funny.

"What is it?" Ike asked.

"This will finally give the policeman something to do. He does not have much work here."

For the rest of the evening, Mary beamed with pride. She wondered how many innocent animals would be spared now that the poacher couldn't hurt them. Was this why the magic of the rainforest had brought her here?

After a quick dinner, Mary ran down to the docks. Alone, she approached the river's edge. She stood on the floating dock, watching the Amazon flow by. Due to the rain, the docks were empty. The water looked particularly dangerous, and was noticeably higher than it'd been the day before.

But Mary hadn't come to check on the weather or the water. She was hoping to find something else. It took a few minutes, but Mary's dolphin guardians appeared, rising from the water near the dock. She smiled as they came into view.

"You're here!" she said excitedly.

Mary knelt close to the water.

"Thank you for watching out for me," she said. "I don't know why you're doing it, but it means a lot. And thank you for sharing your river with us. I love being here."

The dolphins, of course, didn't answer, though Mary wouldn't have been surprised if they did. Just like the rainforest, there was something mystical and magical about the river dolphins. They weren't like the Atlantic Ocean dolphins that Mary had seen most often near her home. The Amazonian dolphins displayed a much more serious personality.

"You're safer now," she continued. "The man who was killing your friends and family is in jail. He'll never be able to hurt you again."

The dolphins came right up to the dock, keeping their eyes fixed on her. Mary reached out to touch them, brushing her fingers against their cool, rubbery skin. Mary half expected them to transform into people, the way that Pepe had described from the Amazonian legends.

After a few minutes, they disappeared below into the depths of the water.

"Goodbye," she said. "I hope we'll see you on the river tomorrow."

CHAPTER TWENTY-TWO

An Unwelcome Guest

As Mary arose the next morning, she immediately ran to the window to check on the weather. It was still raining, though not as much it had the two previous days. Would they finally be able to start their search for the globe?

She got dressed and ran out of the hotel in hopes of finding Pepe, leaving Ike and Helen still sleeping. As soon as she exited the building, Mary almost plowed head-on into Mayor Peñuela.

"Good morning, Mary," he said. "You have good sleep?"

"Yes, it was very comfortable, thank you," Mary said, trying to be polite, yet eager to move along and find Pepe.

"You come with me?" the mayor asked. "I want that you

meet a person."

Mary wanted to politely decline, but the mayor had been so helpful, and she didn't want to seem ungrateful.

She followed the mayor to his office, where two people were waiting. One was a younger woman with heavy make-up, dressed in high-heels and fashionable clothing. Her hair was bleached blond, though it was obvious that its natural color was a dark brown. With her was a skinny-armed young man covered in tattoos. His hair spiked like a hedgehog, and a tiny beard fell from the middle of his chin. He intently fiddled with a large video camera, mounted on a tripod.

"You must be Mary," the woman said, standing as she entered.

Her strong perfume filled the entire office, and Mary almost started coughing.

"Yes," said Mary, unsure about the situation. "Who are you?"

"My name is Sandra Lopez, and I am a reporter from the Semana News Company. Last night I received a call from Mayor Peñuela telling an amazing story of three American children who appeared in the rainforest, and who captured a well-known poacher. Is this true?"

Sandra seemed nice, but Mary felt extremely nervous. She'd never been on television or even done anything like this. But it was something else that filled Mary with pure dread. She imagined Anatoly, still out there and searching for them, scouring the news for any sign of where they might be.

"Yes," Mary answered timidly. "It's true, but we only were able to do it with the help of the Ticuna."

"Is it alright if I ask you a few questions for our news program?" Sandra asked. "I promise it will be very easy."

As the spike-haired man focused the camera on her, a gigantic lump formed in her throat. She started sweating. She looked to the mayor for help, but he just smiled and urged her on.

"Tell her about adventure in the rainforest, and about the beautiful town—Puerto Nariño," he said, deliberately emphasizing the word "beautiful."

A story like this would certainly bring positive attention to a small village like Puerto Nariño. Unfortunately, that kind of attention was the last thing Mary needed right now.

"Is it okay if I come back and talk to you a bit later?" Mary requested.

She really wanted to consult with Helen and Ike first and come up with a plan. She needed a believable story.

"Of course," Sandra said. "Maybe we could meet again in an hour?"

"Thank you," Mary said, relieved for the moment.

Mayor Peñuela looked confused as Mary dashed out of the room. She felt guilty, but refused to stop. She went straight to the motel, burst into the room, and hastily locked the door behind her.

"What has you all worked up?" asked Helen, stretching as she got out of bed.

"Mayor Peñuela called some reporters, and a lady already tried to interview me."

Mary tried to catch her breath.

"Hey, awesome!" Ike said. "I always knew I'd be famous."

"Don't start planning your life as a celebrity yet. I really don't think it's a good idea to talk to them," said Mary.

"Why not?" Ike asked. "They'll probably make a movie or something out of our story."

"And just how do you plan to explain how we got here?" Mary asked.

"Well, I, uhh … " Ike struggled to find a response. "Alien abduction?"

"Exactly! We don't have a logical reason. This could cause all sorts of trouble. What if they start investigating our parents?"

"Yeah, I guess that would be bad," Ike said. "But aliens would make the movie better."

"I'm worried what might happen," Mary said. "If they

broadcast our story all over, it won't take long for Anatoly to figure out where we are."

"Relax," said Helen. "He doesn't know we're in the Amazon. And even if he did, what could he do about it? We'll be home long before he ever finds us."

"He's only one problem," Mary said. "What if others find out about the globe?"

"Why don't we just solve that problem by selling it?" proposed Ike. "No more greedy weirdos chasing us, and we'd be the filthy rich ones."

"That's what Anatoly probably wants to do," Mary said, remembering her first conversation with him in the museum.

"So let's beat him to it," said Ike.

"No offense, Ike, but I think that's a terrible idea. What if somebody used the globe to do bad things?" Mary asked.

"What do you mean?" Ike said. "There's nothing wrong with traveling."

"Maybe not traveling, but what about smuggling drugs or kidnapping children? Someone could use it to murder and dump the body in the middle of the sea, or to get away with all sorts of other crimes. It could be used to—"

"Okay, okay, we get the point," Helen said.

"I just can't stop thinking about how powerful of a tool the globe is. It does great things in the right hands, but in the wrong hands, who knows?" Mary said.

"Well then," Helen replied. "I think we can agree that for now, we definitely don't want these reporters to find out about the globe."

"So, no money?" Ike asked.

"We could still use the globe to rob banks," Helen suggested.

"Helen!" Mary said.

"Relax, I'm just teasing!" Helen said, laughing.

"We still need to figure out what to do about the reporter," Mary said.

"Uh, guys," said Ike, standing near the window and peering through a gap in the curtains. "We need to think quickly, because it looks like it's gonna be more than just one interview."

Mary and Helen jumped up and ran to the window. A boat had just arrived at the main dock, and a huge group of people was disembarking. There were dozens of them, and at least half were carrying cameras and lights.

Mary felt faint, and sat down to catch her breath. Her mind was racing. What were they going to do?

"So now what?" she asked Helen and Ike, who still stood at the window, watching the advancing crowd.

Neither made a sound. Both stared, wide-eyed, as if

they'd discovered an army of approaching zombies.

"What's wrong?" Mary asked.

"It's him!" Helen squeaked out in a strangled whisper.

"How'd he find us?" Ike said, looking like he was about to throw up.

Mary knew who *he* was before she could even reach the window. Knowing didn't make the revelation any less harrowing. Among the crowd, one stood out, clearly not part of the group. A tall, older man with short, white hair and a neatly trimmed white mustache. Anatoly was in Puerto Nariño.

CHAPTER TWENTY-THREE

Making a Run for It

"What are we going to do?" Ike asked, his voice dripping with fear.

He clutched the machete, standing poised as if Anatoly would burst into their room at any moment.

"We have to get away from here," Mary determined. "It's our only option. And we need to find a way to get to the globe without him seeing or following us."

"He'll catch us if we go through the town," Ike said. "Maybe we can hide in the forest?"

"I think it's our only choice," Helen agreed. "But that still means passing through part of the town with him seeing us."

Mary thought for a moment. She knew there was a back

door to the motel. Maybe, if they were careful, they could sneak through the streets of Puerto Nariño, moving away from the crowd. Once clear, they could make a run for the trees.

She proposed the plan, and Helen and Ike eagerly nodded, anxious to do whatever possible to get away. Ike and Helen quickly dressed as Mary packed her things into Grandpa's backpack. Silently, they tiptoed from the motel room.

"I feel bad just ditching the mayor like this," Mary whispered.

"Nice of you to be concerned and all, Mary, but I'm not really that worried about the mayor's feelings right now. I think not getting shot is a little more important," Helen replied.

They crept downstairs, the wooden steps creaking with every movement they made. Mary was sure that somebody, a journalist or even Anatoly, would appear with a camera or a gun at any moment.

Luckily, nobody was there to even notice them. As they reached the bottom of the stairs, Mary breathed a sigh of relief to find the main room empty.

"Let me go first," Helen suggested as they reached the back door. "I'll see if anybody's out and about, and give you a thumbs up if the coast is clear."

Mary and Ike waited, crouching behind a bush as Helen ran across the sidewalk and hid behind a garbage can. Helen peered from side to side, then motioned for them to follow.

Mary was terrified as she frantically dashed across the street. She felt like a tapir being hunted by a jaguar. She reached her friend, her heart pounding. Safe so far, they continued their stealthy escape by crossing three more of the wide sidewalks which substituted as roads in the town. They used trees, houses, and other obstacles to stay out of sight as best as they could. With every step, Mary was sure it would be her last. She could scarcely believe it when she finally stood safely under the canopy of the gigantic trees.

Rain still drizzled from the sky, but the rainforest felt just as hot and humid as ever. Sweat poured down Mary's face like a waterfall.

"So," Ike said. "We made it to the forest, now what?"

"We have to get in touch with Pepe or one of the other Ticuna," Mary said. "We'll need their help if we're going to get to the globe before Anatoly can track it down."

"Uh, Mary, how are we supposed to do that again?" Helen asked. "They're still in the town, and we just ran away from there."

Mary's heart sank as she realized that Helen was right. She been so focused on getting away that she hadn't given much thought to this next stage of her plan.

Then an idea struck her.

"What if they're already out here?" she said, hopefully. "Taremuku and Wueku have been spending more time in the rainforest than in the town anyway."

"If they're here, how are we going to find them?" Helen asked. "We can't yell and scream. We'll only alert the people in town to where we are."

Mary racked her brain, trying to figure out some way that they could get in touch with Pepe and the others.

Ike held his hands to his mouth and tried to make a sound by blowing across his fingers. The only sound that he produced, however, was blowing air.

"Nice thought, Ike," Mary said. "It's too bad that we didn't ask Pepe to show us how he made that sound yesterday."

"But I did ask him!" Ike said. "When I went with him to get the poacher's boat. He showed me how, and I got it to work a couple of times then."

Mary perked up as Ike kept trying. He concentrated intently, continually adjusting his hands and blowing at different angles.

"You can do it!" Helen encouraged.

Helen put her own hands to her lips, trying to figure out how to make the sound. Mary did the same. It was much harder than it looked.

All at once, Ike's attempt paid off. He produced a crisp

and clear imitation of the bird call. It rang out like music through the trees.

"I did it!" he cried out in triumph.

"Good job, brother!" Mary said, genuinely impressed.

Hoping to increase their chances of alerting their friends, Mary led Ike and Helen on a zig-zagged path through the trees. Ike made the sound every few steps. Mary could hear plenty of real birds, but not the answer she was listening for.

"I'm starting to get out breath," Ike said, sitting near the base of a tree.

"I don't think anybody's out here," Helen concluded. "It's no use. Maybe I should try to sneak back into the town and find Pepe."

Mary didn't like the thought of that, but if they didn't find help soon, they'd be stuck in the jungle yet again. Only this time, they'd have nowhere to go.

"Alright," she said. "Why don't you—"

Mary cut off, as a faint sound called from somewhere in the distance.

Ike jumped up and once again produced the sound. Immediately, it was echoed by an identical bird call.

Ike traded calls back and forth with the unseen responder. The kids moved toward the sound, which steadily grew louder with every exchange. Mary knew they were close, and scanned the trees intently for any sign of the Ticuna.

The sound suddenly stopped. Ike made a few more attempts, but they went unanswered.

"What happened?" Mary wondered. "Why did the sound stop?"

"Because, I did not need to answer once I knew where you were," Pepe's voice said from behind.

Mary spun, her heart leaping into her throat.

"Oh, Pepe, it's you!" she said, both relieved and startled.

"I am sorry, I did not mean to frighten you," he answered. "What are you doing here in the rainforest? The whole town is searching for you."

"Pepe, we had to get away," Helen explained. "We saw the group of journalists getting off the boat and coming into the town. But there was one of them who's not a reporter. He's a guy we know from home."

"Yeah, and he tried to shoot us and steal the globe right before it brought us here!" Ike added.

"And this man is here? In Puerto Nariño?" Pepe asked in alarm. "But how could he know where to find you?"

"I don't know," Mary said. "Maybe he found out from spying on my grandfather or something. All I know is that we can't let him find us or the globe. We need to get to it as soon as possible."

Pepe thought for a moment.

"This will be difficult," he said. "Our canoes will take a few days to get to the place where my brothers first met you. If this man travels up the river in a motor boat, he will soon overtake us. We will not be able to hide from him once we are on the Amazon."

"What about a faster boat?" Ike suggested.

"To hire one would be very expensive," Pepe replied.

"But Pepe, we already have one!" Ike insisted. "We confiscated the boat from the poacher yesterday."

Pepe looked confused.

"Ike, this is not our boat. We gave it to the authorities. The town policeman will not let us take it, and the rangers, when they arrive, will no doubt claim it."

"Pepe, I know we shouldn't take it. But this is really an emergency. Is there any way you could get the keys without the policeman knowing?" Mary asked, feeling guilty for even asking Pepe for such a favor.

But then again, this *was* a real emergency.

"Maybe you could use the reporters as an excuse?" Helen suggested. "Go and tell the policeman that they want to interview him. Offer to watch Colin, then take the keys before he comes back."

Pepe looked more and more uncomfortable with each

suggestion they made.

"Pepe, I'm sorry. We won't force you to do something you don't agree with. But we have to keep Anatoly from getting the globe. If he somehow finds it, the consequences could be terrible for the whole world," Mary stated.

Pepe thought about it some more.

"This is a very difficult thing that you ask," he said. "Honor is everything to the Ticuna. But you are my friends, and if you are really here because the magic of the rainforest … "

Pepe's worried face smoothed, and a look of resolve came over him.

"I see how important this is," he said. "We must not let this man near the powerful object that brought you here. I will go and do as you ask."

Pepe turned and sprinted toward the village.

Mary waited tensely for his return. It was taking a long time. With every passing moment, her anxiety deepened. Something wasn't right.

At long last, Pepe came running back. He was joined by Taremuku and Wueku. She could tell immediately that there was a problem. Wueku's eyes burned with anger, and Pepe looked like somebody had just delivered terrible news.

"He is gone!" Pepe announced, breathlessly. "The poacher has escaped, and his boat is gone as well!"

CHAPTER TWENTY-FOUR

Jailbreak

"What?" Mary asked, not believing what she was hearing. "How?"

"I went to the jail as you asked. There I found the guard, on the ground. He was unconscious, and the holding cell was empty. As the man regained consciousness, he told of another, a foreign reporter, who had come to see the prisoner. When he tried to make this man leave, he was suddenly hit over the head with a stone," Pepe explained.

"No!" Helen said. "It can't be!"

"Pepe, did he describe what the reporter looked like?" Mary asked, though she already knew the answer.

"Yes, I asked that question. He said it was a tall, older man with a white mustache."

Mary groaned in frustration as her fears were confirmed.

"We looked for the keys to the poacher's boat," Pepe continued. "They were gone, as was his rifle. We ran to the docks to try and stop them, but we were too late. All we could see was the boat sailing quickly up the river with two passengers."

Mary's world was collapsing around her. Anatoly had helped Colin escape. Now they'd both fled Puerto Nariño on a speedboat. There could only be one reason why Anatoly had helped the poacher.

"Pepe, how good do you think the poacher is at tracking things in rainforest?" she questioned.

"He is a poacher," Pepe replied with a shrug. "His job is to track things. He does not know the forest as well as the Ticuna, but he can find things if he wants to."

"Then he might be able to find where we marked the trees!" Helen said in in realization.

"And maybe even the globe!" Ike added.

"Pepe, we need another boat. We can't let them get there first," Mary said.

"Come with me," Pepe commanded. "We must talk to the mayor. Perhaps he can help."

With Anatoly now gone from the city, the children had no reason to keep hiding, other than to avoid the reporters. They returned to Puerto Nariño and headed straight for the mayor's office. Mary didn't dare enter the city hall with the journalists waiting there for their big story. The last thing she needed was to delay whatever chance she had of getting to the globe first. Pepe went into the city hall alone. Somehow, he was able to convince Mayor Peñuela to join him as Pepe led to the spot in between two houses where Mary and the others were concealed.

"Mary, Ike, Helen! Why are you here? We look everywhere for you. Please, come speak to the newspaper," he said, visibly relieved and gesturing toward his office.

"Mr. Mayor," Mary said quickly, "I'm really sorry, but we can't come right now. There's an emergency. Somebody came to Puerto Nariño with the reporters and helped the poacher escape. They just took his boat and are getting away up the river right now."

The mayor looked confused. He turned to Pepe for clarification. As soon as Pepe finished interpreting, the mayor's eyes lit up with alarm. He made to run in the direction of the jailhouse. Taremuku stopped him, and rapidly explained all that they'd already discovered.

"Mr. Mayor," Mary said again. "The man who let him out of jail is somebody we know. He's a very dangerous person, and we know where they're going. They're trying to steal something valuable in the rainforest, and if they find it, it'll be a disaster for the whole world. We have to find a way to get there first so we can stop them."

She thought about telling Mayor Peñuela about the globe, but knew that would just take more time—time they didn't have—not to mention make their story sound unbelievable. Mary hoped he'd simply accept her alarm about this vague danger. Every second this took was a second closer to the globe for Anatoly and Colin.

The mayor looked back and forth from them to the city hall, torn about what to do.

"Please help us!" Ike begged.

Finally, the mayor mumbled a few words and started digging in his pocket.

"Take this," he said, handing Mary a keychain. "We have village boat, only for emergency."

"*¡Gracias!*" Mary cried, as she threw her arms around the mayor. "We'll never be able to repay you!"

"You are good children," the mayor said. "You make me feel … special."

He smiled, and Mary, Ike, and Helen all embraced him again, thanking him profusely.

"Now go," he said. "Stop the bad man. Please be careful."

The mayor waved them away, and they bolted toward the docks.

CHAPTER TWENTY-FIVE

The Race for the Globe

Mary sprinted toward the docks along with the rest of her group. They couldn't afford to waste a single second. Luckily, they found the boat quickly. Before she knew it, they were skipping along the surface of the river, cruising against the current at top speed.

The wind made the water rough and choppy, but Pepe piloted with confidence, holding the boat's throttle down to its maximum capacity. The powerful motor caused them to jump up and down along the river, like a smooth stone being skipped atop the surface of a pond. It felt more like flying than sailing.

Mary held on as tightly as she could. The wind whipped

through her hair as raindrops and spray from the river pelted her. Pepe showed no intention of slowing down. He deftly maneuvered around logs and other obstacles in the water.

The pursuit continued for more than an hour. They passed boat after boat, causing locals to shake their fists in anger as their own small watercraft rocked violently in the wake. Pepe yelled out his apologies, but they were moving too quickly for anyone to hear.

Mary was worried by the fact that they still hadn't caught up to Anatoly and Colin. Where were they? She kept a close watch, knowing that once they overtook them, they'd need to pass by without being seen. She didn't know how they'd pull that one off. Maybe they could all duck down and hide at the bottom of the boat until they'd completely passed by? Mary searched her mind frantically for a better plan.

"Do you think we already passed them?" Helen yelled, straining over the noise.

"I don't think so," Mary replied. "We would've seen them."

They came to a large bend in the river. Mary stretched to look as far as she dared while still holding on for dear life. Unable to see anything, she decided it to play it safe.

"Slow down as you come around the bend, Pepe," she requested.

Pepe obeyed, pulling back on the throttle, and cutting their speed in half. Mary didn't see anything unusual, but the angle of the river didn't permit her to see much of anything at all. Convinced that the coast was clear, she turned to Pepe. But before she could tell him to speed up again, something caught her eye, coming into view from behind a large bush.

Mary's heart skipped a beat. Instead of sailing upriver, there sat the poacher's boat, moored along the shoreline. Standing there, clear as day, was Anatoly. He peered at them through a pair of binoculars, pointing and waving.

"It's HIM!" Ike yelled.

In a flash, Mary realized that it'd been a setup all along. Of course! Why would Anatoly try to track the globe down, when he could force somebody to lead him right to it? He'd only needed to draw them away from the village. Mary felt stupid for walking right into his trap.

Thinking quickly, she found a small ray of hope. Since Colin's boat was stopped, perhaps they could sail right past Anatoly and gain enough distance before he'd be able to follow. The Ticuna would know how to hide from them after that.

"Keep going Pepe, as fast as you can!" Mary cried. "Whatever you do, don't stop!"

Anatoly didn't even move or try to follow as Pepe sped up. That was odd.

In that very moment Mary finally spotted Colin. He hadn't been in his boat with Anatoly. He was lying on his stomach on the riverbank, holding his long hunting rifle. It was pointed directly at them.

Mary tensed in fear as she forced out a warning.

"Look out!"

Too late. The poacher fired the rifle. Mary instinctively flinched, but she wasn't the target. Immediately following the report of the gun, Mary heard a second blast. Was the boat exploding? They lurched and Mary was thrown to the floor. She landed in a heap with the others. Too shaken to move, she stayed there, listening to the sound of the motor die away. Gradually, the boat drifted to a stop, rocking back and forth in the river's choppy wake.

What happened?

"Pepe?" she called out, feeling hazy.

"I am okay," he said. "But I am afraid our boat is not."

Mary dragged herself to her hands and knees. She pulled her body from the wet floor, and turned, shaking and almost unable to stand.

One look at the motor, and she knew they were in trouble. Black smoke belched from a gaping hole in its side.

CHAPTER TWENTY-SIX

Leading the Way

"Weren't you even going to stop and say hello to your old friend?" asked Anatoly.

Colin sailed alongside the now idle boat where Mary and the others sat stranded.

Mary turned to face Anatoly, whose gun was out and pointed at her.

"Just please don't hurt anyone," she pleaded, knowing there was no escape.

"I'm not an evil person," Anatoly said, acting shocked at the suggestion. "As long as everybody does as I say, things will be fine. Don't worry."

"Be careful about those natives," Colin warned. "They

can be a bit unpredictable. I don't think it's a good idea to keep all three of them as hostages."

"No," Anatoly said. "You're right. That would only cause problems."

He moved his gun to point directly at Wueku.

"No!" Ike yelled. "You said you wouldn't hurt anybody!"

"Relax, child," Anatoly said. "I'll give these two bigger ones a chance. If they jump out and swim to shore, I'll let them go free. Better yet, as soon as you hand over the globe, I'll let you all free. You see? Nice guy."

Taremuku and Wueku exchanged glances, unsure of what was being said. Pepe quickly interpreted.

Taremuku nodded in reluctant understanding. Wueku, on the other hand, didn't want to give up without a fight. He looked angry enough to leap from the boat and strangle Anatoly and Colin. Taremuku held on to his brother, worried about the same thing, and urged him to calm down. Once he was sure his brother wouldn't do anything rash, Taremuku turned to Mary.

"Mary," he said with a knowing smile, "You … magic."

He pointed to her forehead, while chuckling at his attempt to speak English. Mary realized that she wouldn't probably see Taremuku or Wueku again, no matter what happened. She wiped away tears and threw her arms around them.

"Alright, that's enough. You've said your goodbyes," Anatoly said. "Now get out, before I lose my patience."

At that, both Taremuku and Wueku dived headlong into the river, gliding easily through the water toward the riverbank.

"You see," Anatoly said. "I told you I wouldn't hurt anybody."

Mary glared at him through her tears.

"Now that we've fixed that problem, would you young people be so kind as to join us?" Anatoly said. "Your boat seems to have stopped functioning. Perhaps we could give you a ride?"

He laughed as all four of them stepped from one boat to the other. All the while, Anatoly kept his gun trained on them. Colin worked to attach their immobile boat to his with a rope.

"Oh, we can't have that," Anatoly said, noticing the machete in Ike's hand.

He plucked it from Ike's fingers before he could react.

"These are dangerous, you know. Better they stay in the hands of the adults."

Anatoly turned and handed it to Colin.

"Here you are," he said. "A reward for your excellent marksmanship."

"Not a bad piece," the poacher noted, inspecting the blade up and down. "It's a little old, but it'll still cut alright."

Colin tucked the machete into a crevice near the boat's front dashboard.

"Now then," Anatoly said to his prisoners, "give me the globe, and I'll take you to shore too."

Nobody said a word.

"So, you want to play that way?" Anatoly asked through clenched teeth. "I see. That's too bad really. I'm sure you wouldn't want to lose a friend in a tragic accident, would you?"

He moved his gun and pointed it directly at Helen.

"No!" Mary yelped. "Leave her alone. It's still where we left it when we came, in the rainforest."

Anatoly looked at her, narrowing his wrinkled eyes as he discerned whether she was telling the truth.

"So I heard as I listened in on your conversation with Ephraim," he finally replied. "But I didn't really believe you'd be foolish enough just to leave it there."

"It's true," Helen attested. "We didn't know it was there. Why do you think we're still here anyway? If we had it, we could have been home days ago."

Anatoly looked convinced, albeit irritated that yet another obstacle stood in between him and what he wanted.

"What's so special about this globe anyway?" Colin asked. "Made out of diamonds or something?"

Anatoly ignored him. Obviously, he hadn't shared the details of his plan with the poacher.

"And how do you expect to find the globe now?" Anatoly asked them pointedly.

"We marked our trail by carving into the trees. If we find the trail, we can follow it back to where we first arrived," Mary explained.

It hurt to be revealing these things, especially to Anatoly. The thought of him getting the globe and harnessing its power made her feel sick. But what else could she do? She knew he wouldn't accept any other answer. Mary didn't even want to think about what he'd do to them if they couldn't find the globe.

"Very well," Anatoly finally said. "You will find the trail and take me directly to the globe. Do I make myself clear?"

They all reluctantly nodded.

"How're we gonna trust that they'll take us to the right place?" Colin asked.

"Don't worry," Anatoly said. "There are four of them. At the end of the day, we only need one to show us they. They can mess up at least three times before it's too late. I'd say the odds are in our favor."

An evil grin crossed Anatoly's lips, curving his white mustache upward. He wiggled his gun in the air, leaving no illusion as to what he meant.

"So where to then?" Colin asked, looking at all of them.

Mary nodded her permission to Pepe, who in turn explained.

"I was not there, but my brothers told me the place where they were found."

He went on to describe how far they'd need to travel, and the general area they'd be looking for.

"Yeah, I know the place," the poacher acknowledged. "I was tracking a jaguar not far from there a few days back. Almost had 'em too, but then the bugger disappeared on me. Maybe we'll get lucky and find his trail again."

Mary and the others were forced to sit at the back of the boat, while Colin steered. Anatoly sat backwards, watching them at all times, his gun out and ready. Nobody spoke, and they cruised up the river in silence.

CHAPTER TWENTY-SEVEN

One Last Chance

"Is this the place?" Colin asked, slowing the boat after some time.

"Yes, they were found nearby," Pepe replied.

Mary looked around. She wasn't sure if it was where they'd been or not. To her, everything in the Amazon still looked the same.

"Hey, I see one of my marks!" Ike cried out, pointing toward the trees nearest the shore.

Sure enough, a visible "T" was carved in the trunk of a tree.

"So the globe is nearby?" Anatoly asked, focused on the one thing he wanted.

"No," Mary admitted. "We'll need to keep following the marks upriver until we don't see any more. After that, we have at least a three hour hike into the rainforest."

Anatoly grunted in displeasure. Colin steered close to the shore, attempting to get a good look at the trees.

"It's no use. I don't see any more marks," he said, straining for a better view. "It's gonna be hard to follow from the water."

Anatoly grunted again.

"Very well, we'll continue on foot," he announced. "Pull the boat to the shore."

"Alright then," Colin said. "Let me find a decent place to tie off both of these boats if we're going to leave 'em."

Colin continued upriver, searching for an ideal place to dock.

"What's wrong with where we just passed?" Anatoly snapped, growing impatient with the poacher. "You could tie off to that fallen tree."

"Well, it'll do alright I'm sure, but I'm sort of a wanted person in these parts, you see. If a ranger were to pass by and recognize my boat, we'd have more trouble. I just thought maybe we'd find a better—"

"Dock the boat now," Anatoly demanded, with no hint of patience. "If you want to be paid, you'll do what I say. We don't have time to search for a perfect parking space!"

"Alright, mate, no need to get upset," Colin said. "I'll pull her around and tie them off where you wanted."

Taking a wide turn in the middle of the river, the poacher steered in an arc. At the peak of the turn, Mary heard a clunking sound. The boat suddenly stalled. Both boats now floated idly as they drifted downriver.

"What the devil?" the poacher said, turning back to look at his motor.

"What's the problem now?" Anatoly demanded.

"Bloomin' tow rope caught in the motor," Colin explained. "She's stalled. I'll have to clear it before I can get 'er to turn over."

"Then hurry up," Anatoly fired. "I'm tired of setbacks."

"I'll do it," Colin replied in haste, "but it may take a moment."

The poacher handed his rifle to Anatoly for safekeeping as he made his way to the back of the boat.

"Excuse me there, kids," he said. "I'll need you to move over for a moment."

Mary and the others scooted out of the way, giving Colin access to the motor. He fumbled with it for a few minutes, mumbling and cursing the motor as he pulled on the tangled rope. Anatoly moved between them and Colin, continually looking back and forth between his hostages and the poacher.

Mary felt a kick at her leg. She looked to Helen, who subtly gestured toward Anatoly with her eyes as he momentarily looked away. What was she doing? Mary knew her best friend better than anyone, and that tense look on her face meant she was planning something. Mary suddenly felt very nervous.

When Anatoly next looked away, Mary turned to Helen, silently pleading with her not to try anything stupid. But Helen just nodded, ever so slightly, and fixed her eyes on Anatoly. She was a hunter, waiting for just the right moment to strike.

"There, that oughta do it!" Colin said, patting his hand against the motor. "All clear. Let's see if she starts up."

Anatoly leaned over to inspect Colin's work.

"You're sure there won't be any more hang ups?" he asked.

Before Colin could answer, Helen bolted up from where she sat and plowed into Anatoly. She shoved their kidnapper with all of her might.

Anatoly hadn't been expecting that. His feet came out from under him, and he toppled toward the back of the boat. Staying balanced on the rocking, unstable floor would have been hard for anybody, and Helen eagerly exploited that fact.

Anatoly should have gone straight into the water, but Colin blocked his path. Mary realized that Helen's goal was to push both men overboard. Helen's risk paid off. The force knocked Colin from his feet too, and now both men were falling.

Anatoly scrambled and caught hold of a seat, saving himself from careening over the edge. He roared with anger as he strained to keep from going into the river. Colin, on the other hand, wasn't as lucky. He screamed in alarm as he fell through empty air. He flailed his arms in a last ditch effort to find anything he could grab and stop his fall. Unfortunately for Mary, he found her. In his frenzied thrashing, he somehow latched onto her shirt.

Mary stood up immediately to pull away, and quickly realized that was a mistake. The boat still rocked violently back and forth, and she couldn't stand and still keep her balance. Suddenly she was falling with Colin toward the water.

Helen tried to keep her on the boat. She caught hold of Mary's backpack, but Colin's weight from the other end was too much. Instead of saving her, the backpack slipped from her arms, and Mary and Colin both plunged over the side. With a splash, they entered the water below.

CHAPTER TWENTY-EIGHT

Left Behind

Mary was completely buried in the churning waters of the Amazon. She struggled to swim to the surface. All she could see was a mass of brown, cloudy water. After a few moments of frantic swimming, she broke the surface and took a deep breath. Panic washed over her like the waves of the river.

"Mary!" she heard Helen yelling. "No!"

"You stupid girl!" Anatoly screamed.

Mary could hear them, but couldn't see the boat. She tried to turn and follow the sound, but her immediate concern was staying above water. Each time she changed her position, the river pulled her under once again.

"Help, I can hardly swim!" Colin cried from somewhere nearby.

Helen and Ike both continued to yell for Mary, and Mary could hear Anatoly yelling back at them to be quiet. A couple of yards away, Mary saw a pair of arms briefly splash above the surface before disappearing again. Colin was in the same situation as she was, struggling to stay above water in the strong currents.

Mary continued her battle with the unforgiving river, all while desperately seeking the boat. The sounds of yelling voices seemed to be growing fainter. The rush of the water surrounding her made it nearly impossible to hear anything else at all.

"We have to save her!" she faintly heard Ike yell.

"What for?" Anatoly yelled back. "Do you think this is a game? Maybe this will show you how serious I am!"

"Hey, mate!" Colin urgently called from nearby. "Start the boat and bring 'er over!"

Colin said something else, but Mary didn't hear, as a wave of water gurgled over her. Yet again, she fought to swim out of it. Even though she was only underwater for a few seconds, her lungs throbbed for want of air. As she came to the surface, she gulped down oxygen.

Finally, she heard the boat's engine starting. Where was it?

"Take us upriver!" she heard Anatoly snap.

"No!" Helen cried. "Go back!"

"Keep driving or I'll shoot the boy!" Anatoly screamed in rage.

Mary spun in the water in a furious effort to find them. Finally, she saw the boat, and to her horror, it was pushing upstream, while the current dragged Mary in the opposite direction. She could just make out Anatoly, standing with his gun pressed against Ike's head. Helen stared back toward Mary in despair, while Pepe was at the boat's helm, forced to follow Anatoly's demands at the threat of Ike's life.

Mary panicked, and was pulled under again, losing sight of the boat.

"What're you doing?" Mary heard Colin yell as she emerged from the depths once again. "You're going the wrong way, mate!"

What was she supposed to do now? Apparently, Anatoly had even determined that the poacher was no longer useful to him. If he wasn't going to save Colin, there was no chance that he'd come back for her. Nobody was coming to her rescue. She only had two options. Either she could try and swim to shore, or she could drown.

Deep down, Mary knew that drowning was more likely. The current was so strong! With every few strokes, the water would pull her under again and again. She didn't even have enough time to take a full breath before being pulled down each time. Mary coughed out the water that poured into her mouth, and felt her strength draining at an alarming rate.

An idea crossed her mind. Instead of desperately trying to swim to the surface and wasting all of her strength, she focused on not struggling so much. She tried to swim deliberately and correctly. It got easier, and helped her calm down. She was able to keep her head above the water, and finally took several deep breaths. Breathing never felt so good.

In her slightly improved state, Mary cautiously turned in the water, searching for the shore. Spotting it was not a welcome sight. It was probably only one hundred meters away, but it might as well have been ten miles. There was no way that she'd be able to swim to the shore on her own.

Mary felt like sobbing, but she didn't even have enough energy for that. She knew that any effort to swim was in vain. All of her struggling had completely drained her body of energy. She was barely staying afloat as it was, and it was only a matter of time before she'd be swept under for good.

In that moment, Mary thought of Dad. Only a few hours ago, she'd been on top of the world, ready to return home triumphantly with stories of how she'd survived in one of the most dangerous places on the earth. She fantasized that he'd realize how much she'd grown, and maybe even give her permission to travel the world. Now she'd never have that chance.

"I'm sorry. I never wanted this to happen," she whispered to the water.

She looked to the sky and wondered what would happen when she died.

Strangely, it didn't scare her.

She stopped swimming, and the river pulled her under immediately. Resigned to go, Mary didn't try to fight back. She felt at peace with her decision.

"Don't give up! Please, Mary, don't give up!"

Mary heard the echoes of what Helen been yelling just before her head went under. Helen's last plea replayed in Mary's head as she drifted along under the water. These were her last thoughts, and all Mary could think about was how much she'd miss everyone. What would happen to Helen when she was gone? What about her brother? And Pepe? Would Anatoly actually let them go?

I promised I'd get them home, she thought.

Still floating in the murky depths, Mary's lungs started to burn. She'd have to give up soon.

I promised.

Now, instead of getting them home, she was giving up and

leaving them with a madman. She was breaking her promise.

No! I promised!

With a surge of emotion, Mary realized she couldn't give up. Even if there was no chance of survival, she had to go down giving every last ounce of her strength.

Reinvigorated, Mary burst above the surface again, and filled her ragged lungs with air. Methodically, she started backstroking through the water. She didn't even know if she was headed toward the bank or not, and was too weak to even look. Her only hope was that the current would eventually take her near the shore. Every stroke felt like it would be her last, but she used thoughts of saving her friends to keep going. She would *not* give up!

Without warning, her arm struck against something solid. Had she made it?

No, she thought. *It's just a floating log.*

Mary wrapped her arms around it and hung on, hoping to use it to keep above the water long enough to get her strength back. In her drained state, she wasn't thinking very clearly. She wondered why the log felt so rubbery. Shouldn't wood feel hard and stiff?

Dazed, Mary looked at the log, and almost screamed when she found herself staring into a dark, piercing eye, surrounded by pinkish flesh.

Before she could let go, the eye locked her gaze and mesmerized her. She immediately felt calm. Clarity flooded back into her mind, and fear left her completely.

It was a river dolphin! The pink body of the dolphin moved close and buoyed her up. Mary kept her gaze fixed on the dolphin's eye, allowing her river protector to do all the swimming. Before she knew it, her feet dragged along the river bottom. She was safe!

The whole thing only took a few seconds, but it felt like hours. She reluctantly took her gaze away from the dolphin, and with her last bit of strength, pulled herself onto the riverbank.

She heard coughing and sputtering nearby. Mary looked to the left, and to her surprise, saw a second dolphin carrying Colin to safety. He crawled onto the land and collapsed in a heap.

Close to the bank, the two dolphins peeked their heads from the water and looked in her direction. Behind them, the Amazon appeared as a vast ocean. Had she really fallen into that?

Why had the dolphins saved her? Or Colin for that matter? Pepe said their behavior was unusual. What would he say now?

The dolphins nodded, as if in satisfaction, then turned

away, returning to their river home.

"Thank you, my friends," Mary whispered weakly. "Thank you!"

With that, she closed her eyes, and fell back completely onto the bank.

CHAPTER TWENTY-NINE

Searching for the Globe

Mary heard voices. Still recovering, she rolled onto her side and slowly rose to her knees. She looked up to see Pepe, Helen, and Ike running toward her. Helen reached her first.

"Mary, I'm so sorry, it's all my fault," Helen sobbed out as she skidded to a halt and threw her arms around Mary's collapsed form.

"You didn't … know … " Mary tried to say, her words trailing off as she ran out of air. "But it's okay … the dolphins … they saved … they saved … "

Helen clung to Mary, crying.

"I thought you were a goner!" she said.

Ike and Pepe caught up, with Anatoly following behind, his gun still drawn.

"How sweet!" Anatoly said. "I think we've all learned a very important lesson here, don't you? I trust none of you will try anything stupid again?"

Colin rose to his feet and faced Anatoly, anger burning in his eyes.

"Why you low down, no good … You were gonna leave us to drown!" he accused.

"Oh, come now," Anatoly answered. "There's no need to be upset. The girl tried to push us both in the water. I barely stayed aboard as it was. I wasn't able to control them and the boat. But all the same, if it will make it up, I'll pay you what I promised now, and give you double after we find the globe."

Anatoly reached into a pocket and produced a thick wad of cash.

Colin took the money, and held it in his hand as if unsure of what to do. He looked back and forth between Anatoly and the money, before finally putting it in his pocket.

"Alright," he said. "You have a deal."

"Excellent," Anatoly said.

He pulled the poacher's rifle from his shoulder and handed it back to Colin.

"How'd you get out?" Ike asked Mary, his cheeks streaked

with tears. "I thought you wouldn't make it!"

"I almost didn't," Mary answered. "I would've drowned it if it wasn't for the dolphins."

"Dolphins? What on earth are you talking about?" Anatoly scoffed.

"Our river dolphins are the protectors of the Amazon," Pepe explained. "Many legends tell of them saving others, but I have never seen this happen until today."

"It's true," Mary said. "I don't know why they saved us, but they did."

Colin stared blankly out over the water.

"They came out of nowhere," he said. "It was like they knew just what to do. Almost like they were human."

"Well, it is a touching story, but I'm afraid I don't really care. I'm tired of waiting," Anatoly said. "Move!"

Mary wasn't given any more time to regain her depleted strength. She was worn out to the bone, but Anatoly forced her all the same to march forward along the Amazon. Helen and Ike stayed close, and helped her every time she stumbled.

The two boats were anchored securely to a log on the riverbank. Colin reached in to grab a few things, including Grandpa's machete.

"We might need this," he said, slipping it through his belt.

Together they trooped along. There was still some water in the flasks in Grandpa's backpack, which Helen now wore. Mary was terribly thirsty, but she didn't dare try to stop, fearing that Anatoly would take it from her. Mary knew she'd have to fight through this, no matter how difficult it got.

They passed tree after tree with T-carved trunks. They came to a spot that Mary recognized, where a shattered log was lying on the ground. She thought of the grubs that had relieved their hunger a few days earlier. She was famished, and wouldn't be against looking for a few more. If only Anatoly would let them stop.

After a while, they came to another familiar area. It was where they'd initially emerged from the trees, and for the first time, beheld the Amazon River.

"This is it," she said wearily. "From here we have to go into the jungle, and continue to follow the marks."

"How long will it take?" Colin asked.

No doubt struggling in the river had worn him out just as much as it had Mary.

"It took us the entire morning to get to the river," Mary answered. "We still have a long way to go."

Colin groaned, and Mary understood how he felt. The last thing she wanted to do was trudge through the sweltering rainforest.

"Let's get going!" Anatoly ordered.

The group of six entered into the forest, following the marks on the trees as they went.

Anatoly continually urged them to move faster. Mary did what she could, though she struggled to even stay on her feet.

Twenty minutes in, she tripped and fell. Ike, Helen, and Pepe all ran to help her up, but when Mary got to her feet, she realized that Colin was there, helping as well.

"You must feel as tuckered as I do," he said. "Here, have a drink."

He passed her his own water bottle. Mary eagerly gulped, the water helping to cool her parched throat.

"No stopping!" Anatoly barked. "We can rest when we get to the globe."

They walked and walked and walked. Deeper and deeper into the rainforest they went. With every step, Mary wished she could just curl up on the ground and stay there forever.

"We're here!" Helen yelled, just as Mary was about to give up and collapse.

Perking up at the announcement, Mary looked ahead, and could see the remnants of the shelter they'd built during their first night in the rainforest.

"Good, now where's the globe!" Anatoly asked without hesitation.

"We fell into this tree," Mary weakly explained. "We didn't have it when we climbed down, so we thought that maybe it fell to the ground. We searched everywhere, but didn't see it."

"Well, maybe it's time to look again," Anatoly pushed. "No time to lose."

Everybody spread out and began to search. They looked under every branch and leaf, and behind every tree. They searched every possible inch of the rainforest floor within one hundred meters in every direction. But the globe was simply nowhere to be found.

"Where is it?" Anatoly said, his anger boiling over. "You said it would be here!"

"It has to be here somewhere," Mary replied. "I don't think it could be anywhere else."

What would he do to them if they didn't find it?

"It might be stuck in the tree," Helen suggested, seeking to ease the tense moment. "It could've gotten caught in the branches, just like we did."

Anatoly thought for a minute, studying the tree's thick canopy.

"How did you get down?" he asked. "If you fell, you wouldn't be walking again anytime soon."

Helen pointed to the vines hanging from the adjacent tree.

"We climbed down those," she said.

Anatoly walked over and tugged on one of the vines.

"Very clever," he admitted. "But can we climb back up again?"

He contemplated the puzzle, scratching at his white mustache.

"Which of you can climb?" he asked.

Mary knew she wouldn't be able to, completely worn out or not.

"I can probably do it," Helen volunteered.

"As can I," admitted Pepe.

"Excellent," Anatoly said. "I want the two of you to go up there and search every inch of that tree. Don't come down unless you have the globe in hand."

Helen and Pepe walked toward the vines.

"One more thing," Anatoly added. "Every few seconds, you will call down to us. If you even think of trying to use the globe, I'll know, and I'll shoot your friends. Do I make myself clear?"

Helen and Pepe both nodded. Helen took off the backpack and handed it to Mary. She and Pepe each selected a different vine, and began to climb.

Pepe was a natural. He'd probably learned how to climb when he was still a toddler, and with his strong upper body, he pulled himself effortlessly up the vine. Helen didn't look quite the natural as Pepe, but she climbed up without much trouble either. Before Mary knew it, both had disappeared into the leaves above.

CHAPTER THIRTY

The Magic of the Amazon

Mary gazed upward, searching for any sign of her friends. They'd long since disappeared into the leaves, and she could only hear them when they called down every few seconds per Anatoly's instructions.

Helen's normal cry of "still here!" suddenly became a scream of terror.

"Are you okay?" Mary called up.

"I'm fine," Helen said. "I just didn't realize there were huge snakes in this tree!"

Mary smiled. Helen didn't know that she and the emerald boa had already met.

The search continued, and Helen and Pepe's calls grew

more and more distant. Mary wasn't sure what worried her more—them finding the globe, or them not finding it.

Suddenly, Helen cried out.

"There it is! I found it!"

Mary's heart surged with anxiety. This was it. Was there anything she could do to keep the globe from Anatoly?

"Bring it down at once!" Anatoly said. "And don't stop calling to us, unless you want your friends to die!"

Helen and Pepe obeyed, and began to make their descent.

"Whoops!" Helen yelled. "Look out below!"

Something crashed through the branches above. Mary looked up, just in time, to see an object falling directly toward her. She stepped out of the way, the object missing her by mere inches. It hit the ground next to her, and came to rest against her shoe.

There it was, lying in the dirt on the rainforest floor. An object with more power than anything she'd ever imagined. Quickly and instinctively, she knelt down and scooped it up, cradling it closely against her body, protecting it as best as she could.

"Give it to me!" Anatoly approached her.

Mary gulped.

"I can't," she said. "It doesn't belong to you!"

What are you doing? she mentally screamed. *You already*

barely escaped dying once today. Do you have a death wish?

Mary didn't know where this sudden surge of defiance was coming from. It went against everything she knew about herself. She shook with fear as Anatoly stepped closer, his gun drawn.

There was that feeling again, the same as she'd felt in the warehouse. She didn't know where it came from, but an overwhelming impulse to keep the globe from Anatoly at all costs pushed the fear away.

I can't let him have it! she thought.

"If you don't immediately give me the globe, I promise that every one of your friends will die," he said. "There's no way to escape this time."

Mary didn't doubt his seriousness. She took a deep breath, and stood as tall as she could.

"No!" she said, looking him directly in the eye. "I won't ever let you have it."

Mary stepped back, clutching the globe with every ounce of her strength. This unexpected bravery was in control now. She was physically unable to give the globe to Anatoly, even if she wanted to.

"I'm growing very impatient," Anatoly said.

"I won't give it to you!" Mary insisted, taking another step back.

"This is your final chance. I'll give you to the count of three," Anatoly said.

He eyes were twisted with rage.

"If the globe isn't in my hand by the time I finish, I swear you'll never breathe another breath again. Do *not* test me!"

He pointed his pistol directly at Mary's head. She closed her eyes and took another deep breath. The Amazon filled her.

Everything she'd seen in these past days flashed before her. The river, the Ticuna, the dolphins—everything. She felt the entire rainforest watching her. It gave her power.

"One," he counted.

Mary took yet another step back. The surrounding magic fed into her irresistible urge to protect the globe. All fear had completely disappeared.

"You don't belong here," Mary said in a voice that wasn't her own. "Leave now, Anatoly, before it's too late. Just turn around and walk away."

"Mary, what are you doing?" Ike asked.

"Two!"

"Mary, just give him the globe!" Helen pleaded as she watched from the limbs above. "It's not worth it!"

Mary glanced to the right and then to the left. The music of the rainforest danced around her. Her previously drained strength had completely recharged. She wasn't just in the rainforest anymore. Like all those times she'd imagined in the museum, she was in *her* rainforest.

"Final chance!" Anatoly said.

Mary turned and ran. The rainforest floor flew by beneath her feet. She imagined she was a jaguar, and then a dolphin. This was her home, and she could do whatever she wanted here.

"Stop!" Anatoly cried.

The sound of a gunfire boomed all around. Mary was long gone before a bullet could find her.

"Come back!" Anatoly said.

Mary ignored him and kept running. She didn't know where she was going. She simply followed the path her feet found. She was free!

"Ha ha!" she said, leaping over a fallen log and skidding to a halt behind a large tree. Was she far enough away? She tucked the globe under a large leaf and listened.

"Mary! Help me!"

It was Ike!

"This time I'm counting to three for him. After that I'll shoot the native boy, and then the girl. I'll take one out every few seconds until you come back, do you hear me?" Anatoly said.

In an instant, the magic was gone, and Mary's fear returned with a vengeance.

Oh no! she thought.

Mary had been so caught up in the moment that she'd forgotten about the others. Frantically, she snatched up the globe and tried to make it back before it was too late. What had she been thinking?

"One!" Anatoly cried again.

Faster she ran, but with the magic gone, she stumbled over branches and bushes.

"Two!"

No! She had to get back.

"Mary, please!" Ike said.

"I'm trying!" she answered, but her voice was weak and hardly made a sound.

"Three!" Anatoly cried.

BOOM!

Mary stopped short, the sound of the gunshot hitting her like a percussion wave.

Ike.

Snapping out of her momentary trance, Mary dashed forward again, fearing the worst. As she came to the tree, she saw Anatoly, his arm still outstretched toward Ike, as if aiming his gun. Only, there was no gun in his empty hand.

Ike was alive. He stood there, eyes tightly shut and cowering. Confused, Mary tried to make sense of the scene. Only then did she see the pieces of a shattered handgun scattered on the rainforest floor.

Anatoly looked to Colin, and Mary followed his gaze. The poacher stood, his rifle against his shoulder. He aimed directly at Anatoly.

"The next target will be you if you don't turn around and go!" the poacher said.

What was happening?

"You fool!" Anatoly said. "What are you doing? I didn't pay you for this!"

"In that case, let me refund your money," Colin said.

He pulled a wad of cash from his pocket, and flung it toward Anatoly, the bills scattering on the ground.

"I see," Anatoly said. "The poacher becomes noble all of the sudden."

"Better late than never," Colin returned. "But I'm only gonna tell you one more time. Turn and go, or else I'll make you the last animal I ever shoot!"

Anatoly seethed, his eyes like daggers pointed in Colin's direction. Suddenly, the anger turned to pure fear.

"Mary," Helen whispered from the tree. "Turn around, very slowly."

Mary obeyed. She saw it in an instant, emerging through the brush behind Colin. There was no mistaking that black and yellow spotted pattern. And there wasn't only one either. Mary counted four different jaguars, each coming toward them through the trees.

"Don't move!" Helen said.

Mary felt no fear. The magic began to fill her once again, and the steadily approaching jaguars seemed like the most natural thing in the world.

The jaguars were followed by troops of monkeys, who came swinging through the trees. The sound of flapping wings and squawking filled the air. Mary even watched as the emerald boa emerged from the tree, dangling from a lower limb near Helen, and staring at Anatoly.

"I told you to leave this place," Mary said, again feeling the unknown voice coming through her. "You don't belong here."

Nobody looked more shocked than Anatoly. Mary smiled, taking in the view of the surrounding army of rainforest wildlife.

"If you think this is over, you're wrong!" Anatoly sputtered. "Wherever you go, I'll find you!"

He turned and looked directly at Mary.

"That globe will be mine!"

"Not today," Mary said. "And not ever!"

Anatoly looked back and forth between her and the animals. He was shaking. He quickly turned and jogged away into the rainforest, continually looking over his shoulder.

Nobody said a word, or moved a muscle. Colin moved his rifle to point it at one of the jaguars as it approached Mary. She stepped between him and the big cat, gently pushing the gun's barrel downward.

"They won't hurt us," she said, looking back at the big cat.

She stared at Mary for a moment, as if waiting for an order.

"Let him go," Mary said. "He's done terrible things, but we're not killers."

The jaguar nodded, then turned, bounding away through the trees. He was followed by the others, and soon all of the animals scattered, returning in the direction from which they'd come. Slowly, Mary felt the magic fade.

"Great day in the morning!" Colin said. "What in the name of my ex-mother-in-law just happened?"

"You saved me!" Ike said, approaching Colin. "Why?"

"I don't really know," he said. "I suppose nobody likes to see a child threatened. But there was something else too. It's hard to explain. I felt something, you see. I've been feeling it ever since that dolphin saved me. And now all this!"

He shook his head, still utterly bewildered.

"It's the magic of Amazon," Mary said. "It's real."

"You can say that again!" Ike said.

Pepe and Helen quickly climbed down the vines. Colin turned to Pepe, and immediately offered him his rifle.

"Sir, if you don't mind, I'd like to turn myself in," Colin declared. "I've been poaching in these woods, and I'll pay whatever consequence is required."

Pepe took the gun. He was as surprised by this turn of events as they all were.

"What about the money?" Ike asked.

"I think there's a boat that needs a motor replaced," Colin said. "I'll have to pay for that one, and a heap more on top of that."

"I can take you and the boats back to Puerto Nariño," Pepe suggested. "But I will tell them also of the good deed you have done."

"It wasn't me, mate," said Colin. "It's this place! It's like I'm seeing it for the first time!"

All Mary could do was nod in amazement.

CHAPTER THIRTY-ONE

Going Home

Mary felt the power of the globe in her hands. She could go anywhere in the world. As before, the globe subtly called to her, begging her to use it. In any other circumstance, she'd be itching to go somewhere exotic and new. But for right now, she'd had enough exotic and new to last her for a while. There was only one destination she really wanted.

It was time to go home.

"Do you think he'll be back?" Helen asked.

Mary snapped out of her globe-induced trance. It took her a moment to realize that she was talking about Anatoly.

"Probably. I doubt we've seen the last of him," Mary said. "But Grandpa will know what to do. At least we can be ready for him."

"That is, if he ever finds his way out of the rainforest," Ike added.

Everybody laughed. Mary imagined Anatoly sleeping in the dark, eating grubs, and drinking rain to survive. She hoped his experience was as "educational" as theirs had been.

"Shouldn't we head back?" Helen asked.

Mary nodded. It was time. Yet, another part of her felt like she was leaving home, rather than returning to it. Despite all that she'd gone through, the Amazon was a permanent part of her.

Mary turned to Pepe. She didn't even know where to start.

"Pepe, I—" Mary began.

"It is time for us to say goodbye, Mary, protector of the Amazon," said Pepe with understanding.

"Yes," admitted Mary, trying not to cry. "And I'm really, really going to miss you."

"And I will miss you," Pepe said. "The entire Amazon will."

"Please tell everybody 'thank you' for us," Helen said. "You all helped to save our lives."

"I will tell them of course," Pepe promised. "But I believe we must also say thank you to you. I now know that Meetuku was right. The magic of the Amazon brought you here for a purpose."

"But for what?" Ike asked. "What did we even change?"

Pepe glanced toward Colin, who was staring at a line of leaf-cutter ants. He looked like he was seeing the wonder of the place for the first time in his life.

"For one, you helped turn an enemy of the rainforest into a friend. During these last days, I have seen you do things that before I would not have believed. And who knows what else this experience has prepared you for? The magic will continue to work in you, and I believe you will do many great things."

Mary couldn't hold it back anymore. Tears sprung from her eyes and streamed down her cheeks.

"Do not feel sad, Mary," Pepe said. "I feel honored to have helped one who clearly loves my home as if it was her own."

"I promise to come back someday," she said, throwing her arms around him.

"Me too!" said Ike and Helen in unison, as they joined in the group embrace.

"I hope so," Pepe said. "I do not doubt we will see each other again."

Mary turned to Colin.

"Thank you for saving my brother," she said. "I never would have believed it. I thought all you cared about was money."

"I did," he admitted. "But I'm starting to see that there's things more beautiful than money."

He looked around at the rainforest.

"Would you just look at this place!" he said. "I never realized how beautiful it is. I swear, I'll never do anything to harm this place again."

"You see," Pepe said, "only the magic of the rainforest could change you like that."

"You may be right, mate. You may be right indeed," said Colin.

Suddenly he remembered something.

"Oops, wouldn't want to forget," he said, pulling Grandpa's machete from his belt and handing it to Ike. "I believe this is yours, mate."

Everybody finished their goodbyes. Pepe took each of them by the hand, and wished them well in Ticuna.

"Wait a minute, why are we saying goodbye now? Aren't you going back to the village with us?" Colin asked.

"No. We'll leave from here. We can use the magic," Mary said, a subtle smile on her face.

Colin clearly had no idea what to think.

"Are you … fair dinkum?" he asked.

"Come," Pepe said, laying a hand on his shoulder. "As we travel back to Puerto Nariño, I will tell you all about the magic of the Amazon."

"Alright, mate," Colin said. "Goodbye, then, I suppose."

Colin continued to look back at the children every few

seconds as he was led away, urged along by Pepe until they were out of sight.

"Just the three of us again," Ike said. "Right back where we started."

"Well, almost," Mary said. "Are you ready to go home?"

"Do you have to ask?" Helen said. "I've been ready for this since we got here!"

"Me too!" Ike said.

"You mean you're not glad you were able to visit the rainforest?" Mary asked.

"Mary, quit stalling!" Ike said. "Just get on with it!"

"Alright," she said with a laugh. "I'll ask you again in a week to see if your opinions have changed."

With a push of her thumb, Mary spun the glass. It illuminated at once. The surface of the earth appeared in brilliant light.

"Wow!" Ike said, despite having seen this before.

"Since this didn't work out so well last time," Mary said, "do you think we'll be okay?'

"Just touch it!" Helen said. "I don't care if we fall into another tree, as long as it's near my house."

Mary pressed her finger as near as she could to South Carolina, and immediately the globe expanded.

"Let's go home," she said.

CHAPTER THIRTY-TWO

Reunited

Mary watched in amazement as they made the descent from high above the earth. Helen and Ike held on to her tightly. Using the globe was so exhilarating!

She made the necessary adjustments with her finger, and gradually guided them closer to Charleston. Soon, the city was visible, followed by individual streets. The neighborhood grew larger and larger, all the way until they reached the ground. Mary had adjusted so well that they came down directly into her own backyard. Instead of falling as she had into the tree, she landed softly on her feet just behind the Tucker home.

"Much better landing this time," Helen said.

"Thanks," Mary said, rolling her eyes.

"Wow," Ike said. "We're actually home!"

Magnolia trees lined the perimeter of the yard, evenly spaced and symmetrically trimmed. It was so different than the random, natural features of the rainforest. The air almost felt dry. Despite being in the humid South, it was nothing compared the sweltering Amazon.

Am I really home? she wondered.

Mary felt like she was in a dream. Nothing was quite real. It felt like years had passed. Perhaps her experience had changed her more than she realized.

Wasting no time, Mary entered her home through the back door. Her breath caught as she saw was her mother, stretched out and sleeping awkwardly on the couch. Mom had the telephone clutched in her hand, and looked like she hadn't slept well in days. Mary felt a pang of guilt for all the anxiety that she'd inadvertently caused her parents.

"We're home," she said.

Mom's eyes immediately opened, and she leapt up with a scream of joy.

"Is it really you? I can't believe it! I really can't believe it!" Mom cried out, tears rolling uncontrollably down her face.

She clung to Mary and Ike, as if afraid this was a dream. Mary hugged her back as her own happy tears gushed out.

Dad ran into the room, alarmed by the screaming.

"Mary? Ike? Helen? How did you—?" he said.

The shock momentarily froze him in place. When he finally broke away, he dashed toward his children and scooped them up in his arms.

"I thought I might never see you again," he said.

After he let go, Mary held up the globe.

"Did Grandpa tell you about this?" she asked.

"He did," Dad admitted, looking at the globe with disbelief. "But it all seemed so impossible. I thought my old man had just lost his marbles. If not for your email, I wouldn't have even listened to him."

"Nope, he just lost one marble, and a big one too," Ike joked.

"Lewis, I think we should call him right away," Mom said. "We owe him a big apology."

"You're right," Dad said. "I'll do that now."

"Dr. Tucker, would it be okay if I used your phone first?" asked Helen.

"Oh Helen, I'm so sorry!" Mom said. "In all of my excitement, I almost forgot about you! Get over here!"

Mom grabbed Helen before she could protest and dished out another monstrous squeeze, causing Helen's eyes to bulge out.

"Why don't I call Bob right away and tell him you're here," Dad offered.

Mom was still crying, unable to believe that her children were safe and sound.

"Where were you?" she asked. "We thought something terrible happened."

"Didn't Grandpa tell you?" Mary asked. "We got stuck in the Amazon."

"He told us," Mom replied. "But honestly, I couldn't believe it. The Amazon? How'd you kids ever manage?"

"Well, it was certainly an adventure," Mary said. "We tried to call you, but the connection wouldn't go through. I would have written more in the email too, but it was kind of a complicated situation. We were afraid of who might find out."

"It doesn't matter, you're here now," Mom assured her, still showing no sign of running out of tears. "That's all I care about right now."

As they waited for Helen's parents to arrive, Mary told Mom and Dad a little about the Amazon. Both stared with captivated eyes, surprised by every detail. Mary left out the life-threatening parts. She didn't want to immediately turn them against her traveling for life.

Before long an eager knock sounded at the door. Expecting Helen's parents, Mary was surprised when Grandpa entered hurriedly.

"I came as fast as I could," he said. "Are they here?"

"Yes," Dad answered. "But there's something I want to say first. I'm sorry—for everything. You were right all along about the Amazon, and I didn't believe you."

Dad's voice cracked as he spoke. Mary had never seen him act quite like this before.

"It's alright," Grandpa said. "Besides, I haven't given you many reasons to believe me over the years. Keeping secrets is no way to earn trust, and I know I haven't always been the model father. I'm sorry too, son."

"You don't have to apologize. You've been just fine. I'm the one who's been causing this wall between us. I've been angry with you for too long, and it took losing my kids realize it." Dad said.

Father and son embraced, and Mary realized that she would've risked her life in the Amazon a hundred times over for this moment.

Helen's parents arrived soon thereafter, and the ritual of crying, hugging, and expressions of disbelief played out once again.

"So, is this how you always used to travel?" Dad asked Grandpa, gesturing toward the globe, which now sat on the kitchen counter.

Grandpa approached it in silence. He gently picked it up,

his eyes never leaving the object in his hands.

"Yes. For twenty years, I used this globe nearly every single day," Grandpa answered. "I was able to see every corner of the earth thanks to this thing."

"As impossible as it still seems, this really explains a lot," said Dad. "But why didn't you ever tell me?"

"It's a long story," Grandpa replied. "I know now that I shouldn't have kept it from you. But at the time, I did my best to keep it a secret from everybody. The only other person who I ever told was your mother, and she was the most adamant that nobody learn about it. To her, the risk of somebody using it for terrible things was just too great."

"She was right," Helen's father cut in without hesitation. "Something like this in the wrong hands could devastate the world."

Everybody nodded in agreement.

"I think," Mom said, "that we all need to make a solemn promise never to tell a soul about this globe."

Again, everybody readily agreed.

"Grandpa, I get why we can't tell others about the globe," Mary said. "But now that we all know, will you tell us about how it works? I have a million questions."

"I guess we all have a lot of catching up to do," Dad said, putting his arm around Grandpa. "But I wonder if we should save it for another time. Maybe we could let our lives get back to normal first?"

"Lewis is right," Grandpa said, a tear forming in his eye and enhancing its natural twinkle. "But don't worry, we'll have plenty of time to share."

As Mom, Dad, and Ike said goodbye to Helen and her family, Mary caught Grandpa by the arm and quickly pulled him aside.

"Grandpa, Anatoly tracked us down in the rainforest," she whispered. "He almost got the globe, and was ready to kill us for it!"

"What?" Grandpa said. "Mary, I'm so sorry! This is all my fault! How'd you get away?"

"A little bit of luck, and a little bit of magic," Mary said quickly. "I'll explain more later. He's still out there, though, and he swore he'd find a way to get the globe. I don't think we'll ever be safe as long as he's after it."

Mary pulled away as Mom crossed the room.

Grandpa nodded in understanding, but the troubled look on his face didn't go away.

"I'll need to figure out what to do with you now," Mary heard him say to himself as he studied the globe thoughtfully. "He'll be back, that's for sure."

Mary wanted to help take Grandpa's mind off her revelation

about Anatoly. She reached into his backpack, and found the leather-bound journal that Grandma had given him.

"I found this," she said. "It was from Grandma."

She held out the book to Grandpa, who stared for a moment, his eyes glistening.

"I haven't seen this in a long time," Grandpa said, gently taking it.

He held it momentarily without saying anything, then offered it back to Mary.

"I want you to keep it," he determined. "The most recent adventure is yours. Why don't you write about it?"

Mary felt like she'd been handed the greatest treasure in the world.

"I will, Grandpa," she promised with reverence.

Despite the fact that they were all tired, the emotion of the reunion kept everybody up for another hour. Finally, at Dad's urging, Mary was sent to bed. She said goodbye to Grandpa, who departed, globe in hand. Mom insisted on tucking her into bed, and refused to stop hugging her, as if she never dared to let go again. At long last, though very reluctantly, she kissed Mary on the forehead and wished her a good night.

"I love you," she said, before exiting Mary's room.

As soon as Mom had closed the door, Mary switched on

her lamp and sat up in bed. She took a long look around. It still felt so strange. Just as she'd felt in the backyard, something about her room seemed so different, despite being familiar. What had changed?

At that moment, it dawned on her. Nothing had changed in her house, her backyard, or her room. It was her. In just a few days, she'd become a different person. She'd lived her dream, not only visiting the Amazon, but surviving against all odds. She'd never be the same.

As she tried to fall asleep, she couldn't help but wonder how so many people just went about their daily lives, only living in the bubble into which they were born. Didn't they realize what a wide world was out there, just waiting to be explored?

A few days ago, Mary had been a normal girl, living a normal life. Now, she felt like her life was extraordinary. She was an adventurer!

A strange feeling bubbled somewhere deep inside. She could feel new dreams forming, just waiting to be born. Mary smiled as she thought about the possibilities that awaited her. Where would she go next? The real adventure was only beginning!

ACKNOWLEDGEMENTS

This book, first and foremost, wouldn't have been possible if not for the wonderful people of the Amazon Rainforest, who share their home and culture with many, while getting relatively little in return. I give special thanks to the people of Leticia and Puerto Nariño, Colombia.

As this is the first book I've ever completed, it no doubt would have been much worse if not for the insight of many great people who gave of their time and candid opinions freely, including Katrina Anderson O'Hara, Rory O'Hara, Toby O'Hara, Linda Skinner, Ellie Webb, Janet Radford Bergeson, Catie Bergeson Wohan, and Emily O'Hara Bergeson, among others.

A special thanks to the insightful and honest Jessica Ball, who provided a wonderful set of recommendations on how to improve the story and my own writing.

I not only am fortunate to have one of the most talented editors in the business, but she also happens to be a long-time friend. Without the help of Tara Creel, both personally and professionally, I'd still be sitting behind a computer screen, scratching my head, trying to figure out what to do next.

To all those who dream about seeing the world, do whatever you can to make it happen. Not only will it fill your life with bright spots, memories, and experiences, it is the efforts you make to expand your horizons that will literally change the world for the better.

N. R. BERGESON

N. R. Bergeson has been fascinated with the wider world since the dawn of his memory. An insatiable case of wanderlust pushed him to early experiences abroad, and he's spent the better part of his adult life living all over the place, including Russia, Romania, Colombia, Kazakhstan, Afghanistan, and now Indonesia. His day job as a Foreign Service officer has given him chances to work all over the globe, and to date he's traveled to more than 60 countries with his wife, Emily, and their three young children. His love for family and travel is interdependent with his love for writing, and his dream is to instill a desire in his readers to take advantage of modern opportunities to see the world, learn new languages, and expand their cultural experiences. We live in a wonderful world, and it's just waiting for us to get out and see it.

OTHER MONTH9BOOKS TITLES YOU MIGHT LIKE

POPPY MAYBERRY, THE MONDAY

POLARIS

Find more books like this at Month9Books.com

Connect with Month9Books online:
Facebook: www.Facebook.com/Month9Books
Twitter: https://twitter.com/Month9Books
You Tube: www.youtube.com/user/Month9Books
Tumblr: http://month9books.tumblr.com/
Instagram: https://instagram.com/month9books

Monday isn't just another day of the week.

Poppy Mayberry,
The Monday

NOVA KIDS BOOK 1

Jennie K. Brown

Don't open the door.
Don't invite him in.
He is not from here.

Polaris

BETH BOWLAND